~A Monstrous Place~

A Tale From Between

Matthew Stott

Matthew Stott

Please consider leaving a review wherever you bought the book,

or telling your friends about it, to help spread the word.

Thank you for supporting my work.

mrmatthewstott.com | @mattstottwrites

Facebook.com/matthewstottauthor

Cover by: Phil Poole

First published by Fenric Books.

**ISBN-13:
978-1516860395**

**ISBN-10:
151686039X**

For the madman with a box.

Things live between awake and asleep.

In the moment after your eyes grow too heavy to stay open, but before the dreams take you.

Some of the creatures that live Between are nice.

A great many are not.

~Chapter One~

He was awoken in the dead of night by somebody calling his name.

'Billy Tyler.'

He muttered, half-opened one eye, then rolled over.

'Hello, Billy Tyler.'

Billy grumbled and rubbed at his sleep encrusted eyes with the heel of one hand, his mouth dry, as he propped himself up on his elbow and peered blurrily into the darkness.

'Billy Tyler, it's me.'

The voice was familiar and yet not quite right in some way. Like someone doing an impression that was a little bit off.

'Listen, Billy Tyler.'

'Who's that...? Dad...?' He sat upright now, his eyes a little more used to the gloom of the room, but there was nothing to see other than the familiar vague shapes of his bedroom furniture.

'Hello, Billy Tyler.'

No, it sounded nothing like his Dad. Who was it? Why was the voice itching at his memory and yet he couldn't place it? The almost familiar voice wasn't coming from within the room. Even though the voice sounded as though it was being whispered calmly into his ear, he was sure that it was actually coming from downstairs.

'Are you there, Billy Tyler?'

'I said who's that? I'm trying to sleep.' He tried to place the voice. It buzzed at him, teasing.

'I'm here, Billy Tyler.'

'I have to go to school tomorrow, I need my sleep, I've got double maths. I'm not very good at maths so I need to be at my best.'

'I'm here, Billy Tyler.'

He pulled back the duvet and placed his bare feet onto the carpet, toes wriggling. He pushed on his Doctor Who slippers and padded quietly towards the door, opening it a crack.

'Down here, Billy Tyler.'

He wanted to stop, to shut the door and go back to bed, but the voice seemed to be physically pulling him forward. 'I'm probably dreaming anyway,' he said aloud, as though to reassure himself and stop

2

the knot in his stomach from tightening further. 'That's it,' he laughed. 'Just a silly old dream.'

'Down here, Billy Tyler.'

It certainly felt like a dream. Dreams felt completely real and completely unreal at the same time, and this definitely felt like that. Like walking through a sharply focused fog. He reached the top of the stairs and peered down warily into an impenetrable wall of black. 'Down where? Where about?'

'Down here, Billy Tyler.'

'I don't want to go down there. I think I want to stay up here. I mean, I know this is a dream, it's a silly scary dream and I know that of course, I'm not stupid, but I still think that I would really like to get back into bed and not at all go down there.'

Silence.

The front door must have been open because he could feel cold tendrils of outside air snaking up the stairs and coiling around his ankles, trying to pull his reluctant feet forward. Billy wanted to resist. He really wanted to resist.

'Down here, Billy Tyler, down here.'

He stepped forward. And down.

Step by step.

Carefully.

Slowly.

Step by step went Billy Tyler.

He was now unable to even turn his head back to where he had come from, his eyes fixed forward and unseeing in the inky blackness. Finally he reached the bottom. The front door was indeed open a sliver, the moonlight weaving weakly within allowing some vision. His teeth chattered at the night-cool air.

'Out here now. Out here, Billy Tyler.'

Hand shaking, he reached out towards the front door and pulled it open, the wind shaking his pyjamas, toes curling under his feet inside his slippers.

'Step out now, Billy Tyler. Step out now.'

'I shouldn't go out,' he said. 'I really shouldn't.'

'Step out now. Step out now, Billy Tyler.'

Billy remained in the open doorway, body shivering. On the path before him stood his older brother, Andrew. He could see that his brother's feet were bare, water pooling around the soles.

There was an undefined quality about him, a blurriness to some of his features. It had been a long time since he had seen his big brother, who had died six years ago whilst on holiday. He'd run out into the sea, all excited and shouting and full of life, and then—in the blink of an eye—no one had been able to see him. Dad had run in, others too, desperately searching, diving down again and again and calling his name, but they could see no sign of him. The water had claimed him.

Andrew's body had finally washed up two days later and five miles down the coast. An old woman walking her dog had come across him. His skin blue, breath gone. Billy's memory of his brother had gone soft around the edges over time. He'd been so small when he knew him. His sharpest memories were of Andrew's hair, his whistle, the way he ran and laughed. The rest had slid further away, or else were lost entirely.

'Hello, Andrew,' said Billy to his dead brother.

Andrew smiled, or tried to smile. Parts of his face smiled, but others stayed as they were, unable to complete the expression. Like he had forgotten how Andrew smiling actually looked.

'Hello, little brother. Oh how I have missed you. Would you like to come outside and play?'

He already knew he was going to step outside, step towards his impossible brother. He was sure this was a bad idea, but couldn't turn back now, however much he might want to.

Billy stepped out of the house and onto the path.

Andrew opened his mouth, wider and wider and wider still, until it seemed like his whole head was a blackened hole full of teeth.

'I don't think this really actually is a silly dream at all.'

Billy Tyler wasn't at school the next day.

Or the day after that.

Or ever again.

~Chapter Two~

Molly Brown was small and thin for her age; like a bundle of old sticks someone had placed a tatty dress on. Her thick, bushy hair stuck this way and that in tangled eruptions of curls, and appeared to be attempting to escape in all directions at once.

'Why can't I just stay here and be home schooled?' said Molly one morning, sullenly prodding at her cereal as though trying to provoke it.

'Because you just can't,' said Mum, who was used to this line of questioning by now. 'Everyone goes to school.'

'Well you don't,' Molly pointed out.

'Well no, but I'm an adult, and I have to do something even worse than school. I have to go to an

office and type numbers into a computer all day.'
Molly's Mum made a 'yuck' face, and smiled.

'Well fine! But if on the way to school I get
murdered, killed, lost, kidnapped, hit by a bus, or set
on fire by lightning, then just know it's all
completely your fault!'

'Okay then,' said Mum, smiling. 'Now hurry up
with your breakfast, you'll be late.'

Molly wasn't really scared of getting murdered or
lost or hit by a bus. In fact, she was about as brave as
the bravest person you could think of; she just didn't
like having to go to school. The teachers were
always more interested in telling her things *they*
wanted her to learn, rather than things she actually
wanted to know. For example, in Geography, Mr
Handley was quick to talk on, and on, and boringly
on about ox-bow lakes and erosion, but if Molly
dared raise a hand to ask which country had the most
dragons, she'd be met with a withering stare and told
to stop messing around.

The house Molly lived in was ancient, and
perhaps even older than that, or at least it seemed so
to a girl Molly's age. Every footstep was greeted by
the sharply grumbled complaints of floorboards.
Windy nights brought the whole place alive with
creaks and groans, as though it were a wooden ship
being tossed about the ocean as it searched for safe
passage. Molly was certain the house was haunted.
There was no way something so old could not be
chock full of ghouls, but so far, sadly, none had

emerged to try and spook her. Not a single, solitary sighting. Not even when she crept about stealthily at night and leapt suddenly into empty rooms to take a spook by surprise as it went about its ghostly business.

Molly had lived in the house her whole life, or at least the whole of her life that she could clearly remember. The house had originally belonged to her Gran, with Mum and Molly moving in to look after her when she grew too old to be alone but refused to go into any sort of old people's home. *'Oh Molly, they're so insufferably dull, the old; I couldn't possibly spend my final days surrounded by them; I'd go loopy! Well; loopier!'* Gran would shriek, laughing. And of course she didn't need to go anywhere. This was and would remain her home, and they'd looked after her, kept her company, kept her laughing, and enjoyed every moment. Now she was gone, almost a year ago, and so only Molly and Mum lived there.

Molly had never really known her Dad. He'd died when she was little more than a baby. All she had were her Mum's stories and a few old photographs. Often he was looking away, or the image was smeared by a sudden, sharp movement, as though he were actively trying to remain elusive. She wished she had some sort of memory of him that she could roll around in her mind, but no. Nothing.

'He was a good man.' So said her Mum. 'Always helping those that needed it. even if they didn't know they needed it. Funny, too. Always smiling.'

'Funny how?' Molly would ask. 'He told jokes?'

'Sometimes. Well. No. Not really. He was just funny. He'd make you laugh when you were a baby. He'd pull faces and cross his eyes and waggle his tongue and you'd laugh big, toothless, gummy laughs and grab hold of your feet so you rocked back and forth.'

Molly wasn't sure that even as a baby the sight of someone crossing their eyes would make her laugh to the degree her Mum suggested, but she supposed she'd have to take her word for it. The idea that he made people laugh pleased her anyway. That he'd made people happy.

Mr Adams lived next door, in the house to the left, depending on which way you looked at it. He was a proud and rotund man with a bushy moustache and trousers pulled up high over his bulging but brick solid stomach. 'Good woman, your Grandmother,' Mr Adams would bark at Molly. 'Good woman, good woman; not altogether up there, if you know what I mean,' he would say, tapping a red sausage finger to his temple. 'Wonderful, but mad as a box of frogs left out in the Saharan sun. Ah! The Sahara! Now I've some tall tales to tell about that scorched place!'

Mr Adams was an ex-military man, 'I say 'ex', but it never leaves you, the training, the discipline, the early mornings, the cold showers, the ten mile hikes, all up here in the grey matter, ingrained. The army doesn't leave you even when you leave it!'

Mr Adams would raise and salute the British flag in his front garden each morning, loudly singing the national anthem as he did so, medals pinned to his jumper, head right back, mouth wide. 'Fought in strange lands all over the globe, you know; for Queen and Country! Seen every exotic creature known to man, woman or dog; and plenty more besides, things you won't see in any encyclopaedia, or on any of your computerised internet. Creatures with the head of a goose, but the body of a fox. Or was it the other way around? Or the opposite of that even?... Yeti! You heard of Yeti, young girl? I had tea with a family of Yeti once when I took a wrong turn during routine manoeuvres in the Alps. Friendly sort, smell musty like clothes that haven't been allowed to fully dry. Awful tea though! Had to swallow it down for politeness sake.'

The home to the right (depending) housed Mr and Mrs Fisk, an elderly couple who, if she had to guess at it, Molly would say were probably two hundred and seventy years old each. Maybe older. They had both shrunk to the size of children with age, with wispy suggestions of hair scattered atop their puckered, dusty heads. They were always to be found dressed in heavy, thick woollen cardigans and green cord trousers, with checked slippers on their feet, Mr Fisk grasping a gnarled wooden cane that snaked and twisted up to his brown spotted hand with its ragged yellow fingernails.

'Young Molly, is it? I sees you there, young lady!' Mrs Fisk would laugh as she tended the front garden and Molly stomped grumpily out of her house on her way to school. 'Off to school is it? Hm? Good to get knowledge in your brain sponges. Soaks it up like my plants soaks up the yellow sun and you'll grow up right and proper, sure enough. Yes, sure enough!'

'What flower is that?' Molly would ask, pointing out some brightly coloured vegetation in the Fisk's bountiful garden.

'Oh, don't you ask 'er, dear,' Mr Fisk would cackle, 'Hasn't got a clue about proper names and that; me neither, oh no, not us, simple, gentle souls we is, gentle as the sea; we just calls it Simon. Simon the Flower. Oh yes, oh my, we honestly does.'

'Simon?' asked Molly.

'Oh, he looks like a Simon, don't he? Oh I should say so. And that plant there? That's Amanda, and that one's Billy, that there's Big Jim!' Mrs Fisk poked and prodded at each flower with a trowel, naming each in turn as Mr Fisk giggled and laughed. 'And this big bush here, hm? What might you suggests we calls it?'

Molly eyed the large bush that dominated the far corner of the Fisk's stuffed front garden, 'Arthur?'

'Arthur?! That ain't no Arthur; that's Fat Sally! Ain't that so, and correct as well, Mr Fisk?'

'Oh yes and surely indeed! That's Fat Sally that

is! Fat Sally the bush; hello Fat Sally!' said Mr Fisk, finding this funnier than it actually was, if you asked Molly.

Gran had never liked Mr and Mrs Fisk, 'Oh my dear, they are so insufferably *dull.* All they want to talk about is flowers and biscuits and tea and the old days; I want to talk about today. No, tomorrow! An hour in their company feels like an eternity. Once I feigned a heart attack just to get away. Gripped my arm and staggered out.' And Gran would relive the moment in mime, Molly laughing.

Gran's room was still full to bursting with her things, the air thick with her perfumes and powders. Molly would open the solid, heavy wardrobe doors and run her fingers along the row of finely pressed skirts, blouses and jackets; or she might pull out book after book of photo albums, each packed full of the black and white smiling faces of forgotten people. Happy times and places, though a mystery to Molly. She would look at each and make up elaborate stories, imagining the conversations, the jokes, the sounds and smells.

Other times Molly would curl up on Gran's bed and fall asleep, dreaming of new conversations with her, filling Gran in on the latest goings on. Gran would *ooh*, and *ahh,* and laugh at each freshly embellished revelation. When Molly awoke the dream conversations would still feel real, but she knew they were just dreams, and dreams weren't real.

Molly wouldn't tell her Mum about these conversations, because even though she was only young, Molly knew enough not to tell grown-ups things that might make you sound mad; that way led to Doctors' waiting rooms, needles, and questions about ink blots.

In her most recently dreamt conversation, Gran had seemed agitated. She wouldn't rest, or laugh, or feign interest in Molly's stories, but instead kept interrupting, as though she wanted to tell her something. She would start to, but then Molly would find it difficult to listen, to hold on to it; it would wisp and dodge and fade, the meaning lost. Molly had awoken feeling slightly worried, which was silly; how could you be worried about a dream?

~Chapter Three~

'**No** word on that Billy Tyler laddo, I see, hm?' said Mr Adams to Molly and her best friend Neil, who were sat together on her front step playing cards.

'Nope. Word is he's made his way to Scotland to look for the Loch Ness Monster,' said Molly.

'Oh yes, good plan, about time that snooty beastie was brought down a peg or two, oh yes,' said Mr Adams. 'Went looking for the blighter myself once, you know. No luck.'

It was almost a month since Billy Tyler had vanished into thin air. All that had been found was a single Doctor Who slipper, tipped onto its side on the front garden path. He had been in the year below

Molly, so she hadn't known him other than by sight. Still, it felt strange to think that someone from her own school had disappeared.

'The Loch Ness Monster isn't real!' said Neil, pushing his glasses back up the bridge of his nose.

'Ignore Neil. He's got the imagination of a dead wasp.'

'Oi! I'm sorry I'm more grown up than you, but I left monsters behind a long time ago. I suppose you still believe in Father Christmas and Elves, too?' Neil said defensively.

'Course! What sort of rubbish world doesn't have the possibility of Elves hiding at the bottom of your garden?' said Molly, as Neil shook his head and rolled his eyes. Neil was podgy and serious. His parents were both teachers at his and Molly's school- which, yes, was just about the worst thing any child could imagine. But Neil, being pleasingly odd, actually enjoyed being taught by them.

'Good, sturdy lad you are, Neil m'boy, plenty of timber,' said Mr Adams.

'Mum says I'm due a growth spurt any day now; that'll sort me out,' said Neil defensively as he sat up straighter and attempted to suck his gut in.

'No m'lad! Sign of health that is! Just look at me!' said Mr Adams, slapping his meaty frame. 'You need the extra padding when you're out there on the front, I can tell you!'

'The front of what?' asked Neil, wiping a crusty sleeve across his nose.

'Front of what? Front of what?' said Mr Adams. 'The front line, m'laddo! The front line! Where the bally action is!'

'War! Adventure! Exploration!' said Molly, jumping to her feet, cards flying, grasping an imaginary machine gun, ready to do what was needed.

'That's it, you've got it; adventure! Battle to the death! Queen and country!'

'Good versus evil!' Molly was now mowing down imaginary zombie Nazis, who were hell-bent on slurping their tasty brains right out of their skulls.

'I don't think I would like to go to war,' said Neil, slumping down again. 'I don't like to travel around too much. I like where I am. And then there's the food. You don't know what you're going to get.'

'I've been there, on the front line, looking the enemy square in the eye, knowing that each day could be my last. Only way to live,' said Mr Adams, jaw set, his chest swelling with pride.

Molly was now covering her ears to save her eardrums from the blast caused by the imaginary grenade she had just tossed.

'No office job, not for me; tried to put me behind a desk after a while! Oh no, I said, not this fella, you put a rucksack on my back, a rifle in my hand and you point me to where the action is. That's where I should be! Certain death is it? Let me be the Judge of that! I'll grab hold of old Mr Death and give him what for! Front line, girl. Front line.'

As Molly dove across the giggling Neil to save him from the flying shrapnel hurtling in his direction, Mr Adams looked into the far distance, a half-smile on his face, lost in memory. 'Yes. Yes, yes. Only way to live...'

Molly waved at Mr and Mrs Fisk, who were tending the big bush by their gate. Or 'Jeff The Bush' as they called it.

'He's gone again, hey Molly? Hm?' said Mrs Fisk, pointing at Mr Adams with her garden snippers.

'We're on the front line, Mrs Fisk; zombie Nazis everywhere!' replied Molly.

'Zom what? What's that she says?' asked Mr Fisk.

'Zombies, Mr Fisk,' said his wife.

'Oh, yes, yes, yes, I sees, I do. Zombies is it? Terrible lot they is, Molly, worst lot you could ever finds in my experience, 'int that right, Mrs Fisk?'

'He is not wrong there Molly, 'orrible lot to the very core. The things they'd do to kiddies, even!'

'Not right, not to kiddies,' said Mr Fisk, sadly.

Neil leapt to his feet, 'Oh dear, I'm late!' said Neil, looking at his watch, 'It's chicken roast day! I don't want to miss chicken roast day!' And with that he headed for home at the hurry-up, waving back at Molly. 'See you at School tomorrow!' said Neil, pushing his glasses back up his nose once again as Molly pulled off expert army rolls on the front lawn and Mr Adams remained far away, lost in another time and another place.

***

Neil was awoken in the dead of night by somebody calling his name.

'Neil.'

His eyes flickered behind closed lids, then settled.

'Neil, are you up there?'

Neil's eyes open, blinked twice, then shut again. A stone pinged off the bedroom window from outside.

'Neil!'

He sat up, groggy, and blinked into the darkness.

'Hey..? What is it? Who's there?' said Neil.

'Neil, it's me,' said the voice again. It was a girl's voice. 'Come to the window!'

He recognised the voice. Confused, he pulled back the covers and shuffled towards the closed curtains, scratching at his mess of hair. There was a second 'crack' as another stone struck the window pane. Neil pulled back the curtain and looked outside; Molly was stood in his front garden.

'Molly..?'

'Get down here, I've got something really important to tell you!'

'Like what? What time is it? Does your Mum know you're out there?'

'Just come downstairs quickly and I'll tell you!'

'But—' before he could finish Molly ran out of

view as she headed for the front door. Neil let the curtain drop and walked towards the bedroom door, confused. What in goodness sake was Molly doing outside in the middle of the night? On his way downstairs he had the strangest feeling that he wasn't actually fully awake, but he assumed that was just because of how late it must be.

Neil opened the front door, Molly was stood a few steps back, a huge smile on her face.

'Come out, Neil, I've got such a secret to whisper.'

'It's late. Couldn't this wait for school tomorrow?' asked Neil, yawning.

'No, it has to be now, has to be now; come over here, just a few steps is all it'll take, just a few steps, Neil.'

Neil sighed, 'Fine, but then I'm going right back to bed.'

Neil stepped out of the house. It was then that he noticed Molly's teeth for the first time. There seemed to be too many in her mouth, certainly more than she usually had. And then there was their size and shape. They were more like yellowed daggers than actual teeth and they dug into her skin as she moved her jaw. How odd he hadn't noticed that until just now, until he'd stepped out of his home and into the night.

'I don't think you are Molly at all,' said Neil.

'Don't you want to know my secret, Neil?' it asked.

'No. I think I want to go back inside now,' said Neil, and the thing pretending to be his friend smiled a horrible smile and its teeth sliced deeply into its face.

~Chapter Four~

Molly woke one weekend morning, very probably a Sunday, and she couldn't find her Mum.

'I'm sure Neil will turn up, don't worry,' Mum had said three weeks ago when Molly had returned home early from school, eyes red, after her teacher had taken her aside to tell her the news of Neil's disappearance. Mum had wrapped her arms around Molly and kissed the top of her head, unable really to think of anything else to say, because what was there to say at a time like that? Molly had felt a little better, safe and sound in her arms, even if she somehow knew that Neil was gone for good.

After her shouts went unanswered, Molly first

checked her Mums bedroom; the duvet was pulled back and her dressing gown was missing. Molly yawned, more tired than she should be.

'Neil gone, hey? Damn shame, good sort, Neil. Course, when I was in Nepal, people would go missing all the time,' Mr Adams had said, *'You'd make camp for the night, tents up, spot of rum and something meaty and filling to chew on round a crackling camp fire, bit of an old sing-song, then off to the land of nod in your sleeping bag. You'd wake up to find a tent gashed down one side, the contents spewed around as though the tent itself had exploded outward, chap whose tent it was completely missing. No one was awoken by screams in the night, nothing like that, just gone. Strange business. Locals spoke about the Gan'Tach; wild woman witches so they said that would come out at night and feast on a man's guts and what-have-you. Hair washes around them like they're underwater, skin as green as an unripe banana. I heard them a couple of times, oh yes, calling to each other in the night like mad owls. Would sit up till the morning, rifle in hand; no Gan'Tach was getting the drop on me as I slept. It's unsporting. You come for me, you come whilst I'm awake and you look me in the eyes! Manners and fair play cost nothing.'*

Next was Gran's room, but Mum wasn't in there either. Molly swayed in the doorway, resisting the strong, strange urge to climb up onto her Gran's bed and fall back to sleep. To curl into a tight ball and ignore everything.

'He's gone has he? Hm?' said Mrs Fisk.

'Who's gone then, hey? What you talking about there?' asked Mr Fisk, jabbing at the garden soil with a trowel.

'Neil,' said Molly, sat on her front step, playing cards on her own.

'Oh I gets ya'; the chubby healthy speccy boy of yours, hey? That's the one, that's 'im, 'init, hey?' said Mr Fisk.

'That's 'im in one, Mr Fisk. We seen it on the old telly box, Molly. On the news information show, we did. Crying shame it is, young 'un like that, all healthy and full of beans and ready on that very precipice of life, gasping in the future to come, yes. Fair turns the old heart cold and sad so it does.'

'Oh yes, yes, yes; 'orrible luck for anyone that is and no mistake.'

'Oh, don't look at me, Molly girl, I fair feels the tears about to force their way out of these old crinkle cut eyes and down me wrinkled soppy face. I feels things so deeply you sees, don't I Mr Fisk?'

'Oh she really does. Never been one so empathetic as Mrs Fisk. She knows the true meaning of despair. You let them watery emotions out, Mrs Fisk, you don't hold 'em back on our account. You feels it, girl.'

Next Molly had tried the bathroom, but Mum wasn't there. The bath was dry, the shower curtain too. She rubbed her thumb along her Mum's toothbrush. It hadn't been used.

'Mum?' called Molly down the stairs, stifling another yawn. 'Mum, are you down there or what?'

Silence.

Molly sighed and padded down the staircase. 'Mum, you better not be ignoring me on purpose otherwise you're for it.'

Into the front room next, the TV set was cold, unused since the previous night. Then the back room, running her hand along the book cases, stuffed with spine-broken paperbacks. Finally the kitchen. No recently used morning tea mug sat in the sink, no telltale toast crumbs. Molly wondered what was the best thing to do next. She decided to phone her Mum and just ask her where she was and what she was playing at, but then found her Mum's mobile phone sat on the kitchen table, so that would be useless. Should she call the police? That seemed a bit rash. As far as Molly knew, Mum had just nipped down to the shops for milk. She checked the fridge, a full three pints looked back at her. Well, maybe bread for toast, Mum loved a bit of jam on toast in the morning. She opened the bread bin, half a loaf looked back.

Molly felt very worried and very tired. She went up to her Gran's room and curled up on the bed to try and think things through. 'She'll be back soon. Back from the shops. Maybe she's gone to get porridge, or sweets, or a newspaper or something. Yeah, that's probably it. She'll be back any minute.'

Molly felt very, very tired now.

More tired than she perhaps had ever felt.

'Yes... yes she'll.... very soon, I... I bet...'

Her eyes drooped, then sprang open, then drooped again as the fight left her.

And so she fell asleep...

...Molly sat upright suddenly and it was dark. She looked to the bedside cabinet to check the time on the clock. Surely she couldn't have slept all day? As she looked she saw something strange and had to squint to try and make sense of it. The clock didn't have the usual three hands— the hour hand, the minute hand, and the second hand- this clock had thirteen hands. An hour hand pointed directly to each of the twelve hours indicated on the clock's face. The thirteenth hand, the one used to count out each second, jumped about like a crazed fly. It leapt forward eight seconds, then back twenty three seconds, then forward a full sixty seconds, then it would pause as though contemplating its next move.

'Well that's a bit strange,' said Molly.

'Yes, well this isn't the Awake world, Molly, you can't expect time to work in exactly the same way here.'

Molly turned towards the source of the familiar voice.

Her Gran was stood smiling kindly in the doorway.

'Gran?' said Molly.

'Hello Molly.'

'But you're, well... really very dead.'

'Oh, I'm as dead as they come. All rotten in a box under the dirt, dressed up in my best clothes,' said Gran, laughing.

Molly looked at the unusual clock with its thirteen hands, and then back to her dead Gran, stood smiling in the doorway.

'Well, strange just took a step up to really weird,' said Molly, and Gran laughed again.

~Chapter Five~

Gran was stood in front of the mirror on the wardrobe door, fastidiously flattening down the lines of her clothing. 'Yes, well, all in all not too bad considering,' she said, and fussed at her neatly curled hair.

'You're all sort of... grey,' said Molly. 'Your skin, your clothes; even your eyes.'

'Well I am dead now, aren't I, dear? Colour is for the living.' Gran turned with a satisfied flourish and plopped down onto the bed, next to Molly. 'Now what time is it?' She peered at the many-armed bedside clock. 'Ah, I see it's everything o'clock; you're right on time, my dear,' and she hugged

Molly tightly. Molly was tentative at first, before allowing her arms to wrap around her Gran. She had been worried Gran would be cold to the touch, a grey icicle, but no, she was just as warm and comforting and soft as Molly remembered.

'I don't understand this. This is mad. Madder than mad,' said Molly.

'Oh yes, this must seem pretty bonkers, I imagine,' said Gran.

'You're dead, I mean properly dead. Dead as a dodo. How am I talking to you?'

'We've never really stopped, have we? We often natter whilst you're asleep and the boundaries between worlds are at their weakest. It's a bit naughty really. I was told I shouldn't, but then when have you ever known me to do what I'm told?' said Gran, holding her tightly.

A sudden horrible thought struck Molly. 'Am I dead now? Have I died? Am I a ghost?'

'Oh, no, no, no, Molly my love, you're so alive you positively glow!'

'Oh. Well. Good. That's good. Still alive. Okay. Then how is this happening? Where are we?'

'Where do you think we are?'

Molly looked around the familiar unfamiliar room. There was the large wooden wardrobe, stuffed full of Gran's clothing and photo albums, the dresser overflowing with perfumes and knick-knacks, the brass framed bed, the old fashioned alarm clock, 'Well, it looks like your room, your room in our house, but it doesn't feel like our house,' Molly stuck out her tongue and waggled it around. 'Doesn't taste like our house either.'

'Clever girl. We are in our house and yet we aren't, you see?'

'Yes,' said Molly. 'Well no, not really.'

'We're Between,' said Gran, gesturing around with one grey hand.

'Right. Between what?'

'Between Awake and Asleep.' Gran stood and walked around the room, picking things up and peering at them. 'There are many layers to reality. You only live in one of them. The real world, that's what we call 'Awake'. This layer right now exists someplace between 'Awake' and 'Asleep'. Between the Real World and the Land of Nod, where the dreams play. We are Between. Simple as that.'

'Oh,' said Molly, and she found herself accepting what her dead Gran said implicitly. Gran had never lied to her whilst she was alive, why would she start now that she was dead?

'Oh indeed.' And Gran threw herself back down onto the bed with such force that the mattress tossed Molly into the air and she landed again flat on her back.

'I've missed you,' said Gran, who lay back beside her.

'Oh, you have no idea,' Molly smiled back. 'So was there a reason you brought me here? I'm really happy you have, but it feels like there was a reason.'

Gran turned her face from Molly's and looked at the ceiling, 'Oh yes. I tried to tell you as we spoke in your dreams, but things can get so vague in the Asleep. It can be hard to get things across with any clarity. So in the end I had no choice but to pull you Between, where we both could really be.'

'So what was it you were trying to tell me? Something good?'

'Not just tell you, dear; warn you.'

'Warn me? Okay, well that sounds like the opposite of good. Warn me about what?'

'Why,' said Gran, turning her head back to face Molly, her grey eyes steady and serious, 'I needed to warn you about the monsters next door.'

~Chapter Six~

'**They** are very, very old; perhaps even older than that. Our idea of ancient is a drop in the ocean to them,' said Gran.

Molly was perched on the edge of the bed, trying to process what she had just been told, 'But that's, well I mean... no offence, but that's kind of stupid! Mr and Mrs Fisk?!' said Molly.

'I know how it sounds, believe me. But yes. Mr and Mrs Fisk.'

'But, well I mean, they're just the boring old next door neighbours! Wrinkly, weird smelling people, with straw for hair and rancid breath; not monsters!' This was all starting to feel like too much. Between?

Dead people? Now immortal monsters that looked like the elderly? Maybe Molly actually was dead and this weird jumble of nonsense was her brain shutting down. Or she'd gone mad. Yes. Perhaps she'd gone mad. It happened. There was a teacher at school who curled up in a ball in the corridor once singing, 'I'm a little frog! I'm a little frog! Pity poor me, for I've lost my log!'

'Those old bodies, that's just how they appear in the Awake. The creatures here, in the Between, that's the real them. The old couple you see are just a pretence, just the tip of the iceberg; the bit they allow you and everyone else to see.'

Molly shook her head, trying to take this baffling news in and shake out the doubt, 'Okay, supposing I believe you; why do they pretend to look like that?'

'Well just think about it, Molly; who in their right mind would ever accuse a senile and deathly boring couple like the dull old Fisks of being murderers? Of being monsters, even? I mean the very notion is clearly absurd,' said Gran, laughing. 'That's the clever bit, the subterfuge; the pretend-them camouflage allows the creatures to walk around amongst us all, unnoticed, innocuous. Deadly.'

Molly nodded. She supposed she could see the sense in that. A monster that looked like a monster was going to find it difficult to go unnoticed in everyday life, but a monster that looked like a normal, ancient, doddery old couple? Well, who would ever blink an eye at those two?

'Hiding in plain sight gives them the power to pick and choose the tastiest treats for their garden without being noticed, without ever being suspected. When they see what they want, they grab them, quick and deadly, and take them here for their real selves to feast upon, forever disappeared from our reality.'

Gran stood and began to pace the room again as she spoke.

'You see, there is a specific moment, when you're not awake, but you're not quite asleep. It's then, if they're quick, that they can pull you here. Then all they need do is to persuade you to leave the safety of your own home and, well, then you're dead. New trees for their garden. No one will ever know to come here to find you, because no one knows here exists. Even if they did, how would they get here? You're gone, without a trace, without hope.'

Molly lowered her head, a coldness running up her spine, 'That's horrible.' she said, quietly.

'Yes. Yes, it is.' Gran replied, eyes dark as she stood looking through the gap in the thick, lined curtains at the Fisk's house next door.

'You said their garden, trees for their garden; what does that mean?'

'It's... it's not pleasant, dear,' said Gran.

'Tell me.'

'Just like their bodies, that front garden they're always fussing over in the Awake is different here.'

'Different how?'

'You recall how they give the plants names? Paul, Mary, Jeff and so on?'

'Fat Sally, yeah, I remember.'

'That's not just some silly quirk; when they say *'This plant's name is Carl'*, they're telling the absolute truth. You see, those aren't plants at all, not if you could really see the ice below the water; those plants are people. The people they stole.'

'But that's... wait, what?' said Molly. It was a reasonable question.

'It's how they feed. When ready, they take the person into the garden and plant them in the soil; the soil holds them hard, refusing to let go. The monsters then tend to their garden of people, oh, they tend to them with such care and attention,' Gran looked at the floor and swallowed hard. 'The longer they can keep them alive, the longer they can feast on their life force. Their soul, for want of a better word.'

'So... the people are still alive?'

Gran looked at Molly sadly and shook her head. 'I'm afraid not. Once they are in the soil you cannot uproot them. They are dead as far as you or I are concerned.'

Molly knew this was the truth. Somehow she just knew. She wasn't dead, or curled up in a ball singing about frogs and logs, she was Between and monsters were real. Molly went to the window and tried to look into the Fisk's garden, but for some reason, even though it was light, the garden was too dark to see into. A sudden thought struck her: 'Neil?' Gran nodded sadly. Molly looked back to the darkened garden. 'So he's in there.'

'Yes.'

'He's dead.'

'Yes. Well, he's alive, in a way, for a while, but he's as good as dead; there is no way back once you're in the soil.'

Molly let the curtain drop and walked back to the bed, feeling slightly numb as she sat down. 'I mean, I sort of knew whatever had happened to him wasn't good and he was probably dead. But not knowing, well...'

'Not knowing kept him alive. Kept the possibility alive at least,' said Gran. Molly looked down at her shoes. Gran sat gently next to her once more and stroked Molly's hair.

'What do you want me to do?' said Molly.

'You must try to explain all this to your Mother, I can't reach her, which is why I've been trying to talk to you; the young are more in tune with the dead.' Gran smiled as she looked at Molly. 'But my, my; you're getting so old and so very grown up now, that's why I couldn't quite make myself clear to you as you slept. Warn your Mother, see if you can make her believe how dangerous the Fisk's are; tell her you both need to move. Sell the house and go somewhere else, somewhere safe. Anywhere, it doesn't matter.'

'Fat chance of that, what am I supposed to say? *'Oh, hello Mum, you know the boring couple next door? Well they pull people into another reality, plant them in the soil and feast on their souls like a pair of wrinkly, stinky, cardigan wearing succubi'*; I don't see that conversation going well.'

'Then you must try to be more persuasive, make her believe you,' said Gran, firmly.

'Even if I could, I don't know where she's even got to.'

Gran looked at Molly, 'What? What do you mean?'

'I couldn't find her today when I got out of bed. She didn't say she was going anywhere, and she's left her phone behind so I can't call her, or even send her a text.'

Gran stood quickly and closed her eyes.

'What are you doing? What's wrong?' asked Molly.

'Shh!' said Gran sharply, opening one eye. 'I'm trying to concentrate.' Gran closed the eye once again and furrowed her brow, searching; with a gasp both eyes snapped open. 'No! They have her!'

'Who?' and then the penny dropped. 'The Fisks? You mean the Fisks have her? They have Mum?'

'They took her. They don't normally take adults. They're getting bolder.' Gran was pacing the floor, hands pulling fretfully at her cardigan.

'But, no... does that mean..?'

Gran stopped and looked Molly in the eyes, 'No!

No. She's alive. She's still alive, Molly! They have to prepare her for planting first; as long as she's out of the soil she can be saved.' Gran sat next to Molly, 'I'm sorry, Molly. I'm so, so sorry.'

'What? What is it?'

'You're going to have to save her. You're going to have to leave the safety of this house and go next door to get your Mum, and I can't help you.'

'But you're a ghost. Can't you just, I don't know, walk through that wall into their place and magic her away?'

'No, not here, not Between. I died in this house, so I'm limited to this building, I don't exist outside of here. No, you're going to have to go next door, and you're going to have to do it all alone.'

Molly nodded, placing a reassuring hand onto her dead Gran's. 'Don't worry, I can take care of myself, I'm not scared of anything.'

'I know,' said Gran, a sad smile on her face, 'But, oh, Molly, it's going to be more dangerous than I can tell you, but if you don't go next door then your Mother will go into the soil and then there will be nothing you or I or anyone else can do. The Fisks will eat her alive.'

~Chapter Seven~

Molly stepped out of her house and the sudden silence caused her to hold her breath. It wasn't a normal silence. It was quieter than that and she shuddered despite herself.

'Do not deviate,' Gran had warned her. *'Do not look around. Do not go anywhere else other than directly next door and into that foul house. Find your Mother and bring her back here. You bring her back to the safety of this house. Between is not to be trusted, not to be taken lightly. Everything out there can be dangerous and it's so very easy to become lost. The streets don't always just stay where they are like in the Awake. Quickly my dear, be safe, be safer than that even, and good luck.'*

Molly looked out onto the street; it seemed so normal, like she could actually have stepped back into the real world, but as she looked closer the differences became apparent. They were mostly small and subtle, a different coloured front door here, too many windows on a house there; it was like someone had made a copy in haste and hadn't had time to go back to check for mistakes.

'There's no one here and nothing that can hurt me,' Molly said, hoping that saying a lie out loud would fool her body into going where it needed to go. She took a couple of steps forward onto the garden path, and glanced back up at her Gran's bedroom window, hoping to see her looking down with an encouraging smile. The window was empty.

Molly moved towards the gate, looking over to the Fisks' front garden on her right; it looked completely alien to how it appeared in the real world, threatening even. She squinted to try and more clearly see what it was that was so wrong, but somehow the garden seemed to be in another time of day, draped in night, too dark to see anything sharply. Even so, Molly could see that the garden wasn't the normal jumble of flowers, small trees and bushes; the black shapes planted here were larger, stranger, and bulged, fighting for space. She realised she was suddenly nauseous and looked away from the garden, fighting back the queasiness.

'Don't be such a baby!' said Molly. That's when she noticed the Boy in the window.

39

He was about six years old and looked relieved when he realised his frantic waving had caught Molly's attention. He started mouthing words; Molly guessed he was probably shouting and wondered what she should do. She knew she had to go next door. She had to face whatever was in there and save her Mum. She didn't have time for distractions. Then again, this was a little kid who seemed to be in trouble, and her Mum was an adult; she'd be furious if Molly had let something happen to a child because of her.

Molly approached the Boy waving from the house opposite and gave him a wave back. 'What is it? Are you alright?' she asked, as the Boy continued to silently shout and wave his skinny arms around. She crossed the road and stepped up onto the pavement. 'Hey, what is it? What's wrong with you?'

As she moved closer to the house she began to be able to make out his muffled cries: 'Help me! Please help, he locked me in and I can't get out!'

'What? Who did?'

'Please, you've got to let me out!' the Boy shouted frantically.

'Okay, okay!' Molly snapped. 'Is anyone else in there with you?'

'No, let me out, I'm all on my own and I'm scared!'

'Right, in that case you can wait. I have to go into the house over there with the weird garden and get my Mum. You'll be fine in there till I get back, yes?' and with that Molly turned to move off—

'Please! No! He might come back any second. You have to let me out now! Now, now, now!' screamed the Boy, causing Molly to stop and turn back.

'Look, my Mum is in danger-'

'They're not in there!'

'What? Who isn't in there?'

'The old two, they're always out at this time, don't come back for hours and hours, so you see you've got time to let me out and then go over, loads of time! Please, I'm so scared! And... I need the toilet.'

Molly sighed, torn between the two houses. She peered at the Fisks' house, trying to make out any signs of life, any movement or light from within that would mean the Boy was lying; but as before, the strange gloom shrouding the place prevented any clarity.

'You're sure they're definitely out?' asked Molly.

'Very sure, yes, yes, very sure!' said the Boy, nodding eagerly.

'Because if they're not I'll give you a smack and stick you back in there and throw away the key, you hear me? That's a promise and I don't break promises!'

'Cross my heart and hope to die!' shouted the Boy, placing a hand over his heart.

Molly grunted and kicked at the pavement,

'Okay, fine, wait there.' Molly took one last look over at the Fisks', then turned towards the Boy's house. As she did so, she thought she glimpsed a figure at the far end of the road. Although she only saw it for half a second, less even than that, she knew it was a man, unnaturally tall, dressed all in black. When she looked back, the man was nowhere to be seen. Molly hurried to the front door, which she found was open a crack, and pushed her way quickly inside.

The air within the house was stale and lazy, like nothing had moved in there for a long time. Years, perhaps, though Molly knew that couldn't be true. The Boy upstairs couldn't have been locked in that room for very long. He'd have died. She had never been inside this house, at least, not in the real world. The Awake world. It belonged to a young married couple who never seemed to actually be in, they were always on their way out somewhere, dressed up and laughing at the centre of a gaggle of friends. Mum said they were dancers. Molly just thought they were loud and annoying. She didn't know much else about the annoying couple, though she did know one other thing for sure— they didn't have a child, which made her wonder who exactly the trapped boy upstairs was.

'Hey, are you okay up there?' Molly shouted as she reached the foot of the stairs.

'Please hurry!' came the Boy's muffled reply.

Molly made her way up the white carpeted stairs,

each step creaking its complaint beneath her foot as she stepped on it. About halfway up something caught her eye and made her stop. On the step in front of her was a single, dark red footprint, dried into the fibres.

'Quickly, please, I'm scared!' shouted the Boy.

'Wait a second!' Molly crouched to peer closer at the footprint. Perhaps it was paint? Somehow she knew it wasn't though. Somehow she knew very well that it was blood. 'Oh. Hey, is there anything I should know? Anyone else in here?'

'No! I'm all alone, always all alone and so very scared, please let me out, please!'

Molly stepped gingerly over the bloodied step and onto the one above. She went the rest of the way more carefully, looking for further bloody prints, but the carpet shone white and clean. At the top of the stairs she had to turn into a corridor. The light was off and it was difficult to see. Molly felt about on the wall for a light switch-

'Please help, quickly, quickly!' begged the Boy, his voice more clear now.

'Okay, okay, wait a second will you!' snapped Molly as her hand finally found the switch, 'Ah—!' she pressed it and the corridor was suddenly swamped with light, 'Oh...' Any further words were lost as she took in what had been hidden in the dark: prints. Lots and lots of prints. Footprints and handprints. Just like on the stairs they were dark red due to age, but this time it wasn't just a solitary print. They were everywhere. They covered the white carpet, crisscrossing over the walls to the left and right, and all over the ceiling too; hundreds of them, thousands even. The air hung heavy with a metallic tang, and Molly felt the urge to run back down the staircase and into the street swell in her stomach.

'What's happening? Please let me out, oh please!' begged the Boy in the room.

'What... what's with all the prints?'

'Prints? I don't know no prints, please hurry.'

Molly swallowed and stepped forward onto the crispy, bloodstained carpet, making her way towards the blue door at the end of the corridor. She passed an open door to her right and looked inside; it was completely destroyed, the furniture smashed to splinters, a mattress torn to shreds, and everywhere the dark red prints.

'What happened here, exactly? Feel free to say nothing at all worrying or scary.'

'What happened where? Why are you taking so long? It's not a long corridor, please hurry, I'm so scared, I need to get out.'

As Molly reached the blue door at the end she noticed there was a note pinned to it. The paper was old, brown with age and ragged at the edges. In clear, ornately written block capitals in dark purple ink, it read simply:

'Do Not Let The Boy Out. He Is Bad And A Liar.'

'What's this note mean exactly?' asked Molly.

'What note? I can't see through doors, can I? Now turn the handle and push!' snapped the Boy.

'It says not to let you out. Says you're bad and a liar.'

'Hey, I'm not a liar! I always tell the truth, me, because I'm a really good boy and a credit to my Mum and Dad!' said the Boy indignantly.

'Well, that's exactly what a liar would say, if they were a liar and someone was trying to make out whether they were or not.' The Boy was silent. 'Well?'

'I'm only a little boy,' he whimpered, 'Open the door please, I'm hungry. And thirsty. I had to take a wee in the corner.'

'Oh yuck...' said Molly, wrinkling up her face. She touched the large, round metal handle. It was ice cold beneath her fingertips. She looked at the empty key hole beneath. 'Hey, there's no key in the door, how can I unlock it?'

'Don't need no key, do you? It's not locked, turn the handle! Turn the handle!' the Boy shouted, impatiently.

'What? I don't understand. Why can't you get out if the door isn't locked?' asked Molly, taking a step back. Something told her that the very last thing she should do was open that door.

'Isn't it obvious?' said the Boy.

'Not really, why don't you tell me something completely believable and then I'll see if I believe it.'

'Well, it's 'cos... I'm tied up. I'm on the bed, ropes round my arms and legs. Oh, he was so mean and awful and bad to me, a poor little boy! I cried and shouted for him not to tie me up, but he didn't care, he's the bad one!'

'Ah, that makes sense.'

'Yes! See? All makes sense, all right as rain! Now open the door. I'm really very scared,' said the Boy, delight in his voice now.

'One little thing though, you were over by the window, waving at me. I may be being stupid, but how did you do that if you were all tied up on the bed?'

Silence.

'You know, these prints are pretty small,' said Molly, looking closer at the red smears covering the wall next to her. 'I don't think a grown up made these. They look like a kid did them. Quite a small kid, too. Are these your prints?'

Silence.

Molly banged on the door. 'Oi, I asked you a question! Did you leave all these blood prints everywhere?'

The Boy giggled.

It was a high-pitched giggle and it slid out of the room like a razor, Molly wincing.

'I think maybe I won't let you out after all,' said Molly, and she stepped back.

The door shook furiously as something very strong punched and barged and kicked at it; but it remained steadfastly shut. 'Open! Open the door, stupid girl, open now or I'll make patterns on the walls with your blood too, stupid idiot selfish girl!' screamed the Boy.

'You're not really convincing me there. I think you can stay right where you are; whoever put you in there had the right idea.'

'I'm going to pull you into bits, stupid ugly girl! Going to open you up and do my painting! D'you like my painting, stupid, stinking girl? Open! Open! Open—!'

The screaming, threat-filled tantrum grew more muffled as Molly made her way quickly back along the bloodstained corridor, down the stairs, and headed for the front door, angry with the strange lying Boy, but much more angry with herself, that she'd let herself be distracted from her mission; well, no more. She would walk straight out of this house and head for whatever waited at the Fisks'; she would save her Mum and nothing and no one was going to stop her n...

... the thought remained unfinished in her head as Molly stepped out of the house that stood directly opposite her own and strode into the front garden. Only it wasn't that home's front garden, with its neat, round bushes and empty ceramic pots; this one was completely paved over, a large red car sat to her left, and the street beyond the gate (which was now brown and wooden rather than twisted iron painted green) was not her street at all. It was a completely different street.

Molly looked back to the house she had just stepped out of, to find that it too had now changed. She hadn't a single clue as to where she was.

~Chapter Eight~

Molly tried to re-enter the house, which was now a completely different house to the one she had walked out of, but the door was locked. She knocked, rang the bell, bashed at the window, but no one came to answer. She picked up a rock and thought about smashing one of the windows and climbing in, but even if she did, what then? Would the house inside suddenly be the one imprisoning the Boy again, or would she just find herself inside this new house and still be as lost as ever? Molly threw the rock into the street in anger and sat on the front step, absolutely incandescent with rage at herself.

The note had told the truth, the Boy was bad and

a liar. That being the case, how did she know if he'd told the truth about the Fisks having gone out, and that they would be out for hours? Perhaps they had been in their house all along, and now it was much too late and her Mum was dead, all because of her stupidity.

Molly jumped to her feet and screamed out in impotent anger. As she stopped to catch her breath, someone screamed in reply.

It had sounded almost like an animal, a beast, perhaps a wolf. But Molly knew that it wasn't any of those, it was a person. She moved slowly to the gate and looked to her left, the direction of the scream. At first she thought the street was empty, then she blinked and there he was. It was the unnaturally tall man in black she'd glimpsed on her way into the lying Boy's house.

The man was quite still and he almost seemed like he wasn't really there at all, like he'd been superimposed, or badly Photoshopped into the picture. Molly could hear her heartbeat pounding furiously. 'Hey! Are you trying to scare me? Because it won't work, alright?' Molly screamed with much more authority than she felt. The tall man said nothing and did nothing. Molly felt a bit better, she'd told that creep what for.

And then the tall man began to walk.

He began to walk towards Molly.

Molly pulled open the gate and moved out into the street, 'Hey, you just stay where you are, okay?'

Long, steady strides, the tall man took; he was in no hurry.

'Are you listening to me? Stay back or else, you weirdo!'

Forward he came, he didn't pause and didn't turn away.

Molly spotted a bicycle propped up against the hedge of the house next door. It was a bit too small for her but it would have to do. She leapt onto it and pedalled furiously to the bottom of the street, turning sharply into the next street, and then the next street, and the one after that. She rode until her throat felt wind-chapped and her thighs ached and she thought she might throw up. Finally she stopped and shakily stepped off the bike, her breathing quick and hungry. She walked wobbly-legged onto the pavement and pushed her way into a garden with an overgrown hedge, dragging the liberated bicycle behind her, before collapsing onto the ragged lawn, gasping for air.

The tall man had been left long behind, she was sure of that; she'd glanced over her shoulder every few seconds and there'd been no sign of him. In fact, there'd been no sign of anyone. Street after street after street, empty.

Feeling better composed now, she sat up and pondered her situation. She still had no idea where she was. None of the streets she rode down had looked at all familiar. Then she remembered her phone.

She patted at her pockets, and there it was, a small lump of plastic, five years out of date because Mum would only let her use one of her old ones. She'd only let her have it in the first place to keep safe. Who to call? Perhaps if she called her house Gran would answer? She dialled the number and put the phone to her ear. It rang twice, then crackled to such a painful degree that Molly pulled it away from her ear in surprise.

'Hello?'

The voice creeped quietly out of the phone, Molly quickly put it back to her ear. 'Gran? Hello, Gran, is that you?'

'No.' The voice was male, emotionless.

'Oh. Who is this? Are you at my house?'

'I am not in a house. I am in a street,' replied the voice flatly.

'But I phoned home. How did you pick up?'

'What are you doing Between?' asked the voice.

'None of your business, whoever you are.'

'You spoke to the lying boy in the room. What were you talking about?'

Molly felt the hairs on the back of her neck prickle. 'It's you. You're the tall man in black.'

'Yes.'

'What do you want?'

'I want to know where you are. Then I can also be there.'

'Tough!' Molly hung up the phone quickly, her heart racing. This was bad, there was no doubt about it. She was lost and alone with a stranger chasing after her and no way of knowing how to get back to her street. Was she even in her own town anymore? Her own country? How did things work here? Perhaps she'd never find a way ba—

DING-DING!

Molly jumped at the sudden, shrill noise and looked up to see that a red double-decker bus was parked in front of the house. She had neither seen nor heard any sign of its approach, but now there it was. One thing was for sure; it was a British bus, so she was, at the very least, still in the same country.

DING-DING!

The doors hissed open to reveal the driver, who was so large and round that it was as though he was one with his driver compartment itself. His face was speckled with random outcrops of whiskers, and his eyes were so close together that a single hard sneeze might cause them to collapse into one.

'Well?' said the Driver. 'Getting on or staying put?'

'Do you go by Whitmore Avenue?' Molly asked.

'We go everywhere,' said the Driver.

Molly stepped onto the bus. 'Oh,' She patted at her pockets. 'I don't think I have any money.'

'Money?' And the Bus Driver laughed. 'Take a seat young girl.'

The doors closed with a sigh and the Driver gave the bell a quick 'ding' before he eased the bus away from the pavement, and off they went.

The interior of the bus was gloomy and strangely dank, the shapes of other passengers indistinct, but Molly could see that the bus was almost full.

She took one faltering step forward into the silent interior and peered at the nearest passenger. It was a man. Or it had been a man, once upon a time. His eyes, now shrunken and dry, hung from their sockets. His tongue lolled fatly from a breathless mouth with what remained of his broken, brown teeth framing it. He was dead. They were all dead. Every single passenger was a corpse.

The Driver laughed and hit the bell over and over in delight. 'Welcome, to the bus of the dead; this will be your final destination!'

~Chapter Nine~

Molly staggered backwards towards the driver, 'Stop! Stop the bus, I want off!'

'Stop the bus?' said the Driver, 'Between officially designated stops? Oh no, more than my jobs worth.'

'They're all dead... all of them!'

The Driver licked his lips with a sharp black tongue that was split at the end into two prongs that moved independent of each other.

'Oh yes, they have all reached their final destination, thanks to me. I always get them where they're going. Don't you worry girl; I'll do the same for you too.'

Molly banged on the plastic door to the Driver's compartment, 'You better let me off right now or I'll, well, I'll do something horrible to you-!' she raised her small fists by way of a show of force, chin out, mouth a grim line. The Driver hit the brake, causing Molly to tumble to the grimy floor as the bus doors hissed open.

'Good! You're lucky you did as I asked 'cause otherwise I'd have...' Molly's voice died in her throat as a dirty black boot stomped onto the bus, followed by a second. She looked up from her place on the floor, up to a man in a tatty, ancient bus conductor's uniform. His cheeks were sunken, his lips missing to reveal a permanent skeletal grin, and his eyes were hidden in shadow beneath the brim of his frayed hat.

'Tickets, please,' came a voice like nails on a chalk board. 'Show me your tickets please.'

'Better do as he says, girl, or you're for it,' said the Driver, and he chuckled, his face eager, unnatural black tongue darting from his mouth.

'Tickets, please. Show me your valid tickets for this journey.'

'I don't have a ticket, he didn't give me any ticket!' said Molly.

'They always blame the driver,' said the Driver, sadly shaking his head.

'Ticket please.' said the Conductor again, advancing on Molly. She scrabbled up to her feet and looked for a way out, but the Conductor's frame blocked the exit.

'I said I don't have one! What're you going to do, hey? Tell the police?'

The Driver laughed at that, a proper belly laugh, 'Police? That's good that; oh that's proper rich!'

'Tickets, please. Please show me your valid ticket.' and the Conductor pulled a large, rusted blade from his coat pocket. It looked like an old bayonet, the kind of knife they attached to the tops of guns in World War One.

'What are you doing? Hey! Put that down—'

The Conductor swung it at Molly's head, narrowly missing as she ducked. 'Tickets please.'

She ducked a second time, and a third, then bolted for the narrow staircase, scrabbling upwards on hands and knees.

'Tickets please.' The Conductor followed, steadily taking each step upwards.

Like downstairs, the top floor was full of the dead, no doubt the work of the Conductor and his rusty blade.

'Tickets. Tickets, please.'

The Conductor was still out of sight as he slowly stalked his way up the winding stairs. Molly desperately looked around for a way out; she spotted two of the dead leant forward in their seats. She dove behind them, flattening herself against the seat, and heaved the corpses towards her so that their bodies and tattered coats masked her presence, doing her best to block out the rancid smell that forced its unwanted way up her nostrils.

Two heavy boots stepped onto the top deck. 'Tickets please.'

Molly held her breath.

Silence.

Very slowly, she moved her head. Just slightly. She peered with one eye through a button hole in one of the corpses coats; the Conductor had his back to her. His head slowly swung from one side of the bus to the other, searching.

'Tickets please.' He slowly dropped down to one knee, his movements stiff and awkward. He placed one palm against the floor and bent further, looking along the length of the bus, first one way, then the next. Molly knew he was looking for a small girl, balled up under a seat; but all he would see was old shoes and newspapers. The Conductor straightened, then stood again, joints cracking.

He seemed to waver, considering his next move, before swiftly twisting to one side and thrusting his blade into one of the seated corpses with such force that it stabbed into the seat itself. 'You must show a valid ticket.' And the next one, through went the blade, brittle, dead bones yielding with a terrible crack as he went about his business. The conductor was making his way methodically from one corpse to the next, stabbing until he found the bodies that hid her.

Molly began to breathe slowly. Steady, shallow, so the body in front of her remained still. She knew she was in bad trouble, her only chance was to make a run for the stairs once the Conductor had made his way to the far end of the bus. Push the body and race down the stairs, pull the door aside and jump for it.

But then the Conductor stopped, and he turned.

He turned back towards where Molly hid, now once again holding her breath. Had she made a noise? The air moving in and out of her lungs too heavy?

'Tickets. Tickets please.' The Conductor made his way down towards where she hid. He stopped two seats from her, the rusted blade thrusting through the body of a dead woman. He didn't know, he was still guessing, but he was so close now, and he was between Molly and the stairs. She was trapped.

'Tickets.' He stopped before the seats in front of where Molly hid, sticking the knife into the corpse who sat there with such force that it stuck right through the back of the seat, the pointed end just touching the clothing of one of the bodies she lay behind.

'Last chance, tickets please.' The Conductor stepped forward, he held the blade high, his dried face with its fraying skin blank and without mercy. 'I said tickets plea—'

Screaming with a mix of fury and effort, Molly thrust her arms forward, propelling the top half of the corpse she hid behind towards the Conductor, its legs remaining stuck to the seat. The body's head struck the Conductor in the throat and he staggered back, his bayonet clattering to the floor.

Molly leapt from the seat. Seeing the blade fall she ducked and grabbed it, the Conductor recovering enough to swing a large fist in her direction, but Molly was quicker, ducking the lumbering blow then striking upward with the blade, sinking it deeply into the Conductor's arm.

He made no sign of being in pain, but it was enough for him to take a couple of steps backwards. Taking advantage of the Conductor's momentary loss of balance, Molly, blade still in hand, sprinted past him and towards the staircase, running down each step with such speed that her foot missed half-way down and she fell the rest of the way, landing in a painful heap at the bottom.

The bus screeched to a halt as the Driver pushed the brakes in surprise. 'What's happening back there? I'll have no monkey business on my bus!'

Molly leapt up, blade still in hand, as the Driver emerged from his compartment. His eyebrows shot up in surprise as he saw Molly stood before him, face like thunder, knife in hand.

'Open that door, right now, or you're going to find yourself with a puncture.'

'But this is not a designated stop.'

'Tickets... please...'

Molly glanced up the stairs as the Conductor's heavy boots stomped onto the first step. She stepped towards the Driver, waving the rusty blade. 'Right now! Open the doors!'

The Driver glanced to the stairs as the heavy steps made their way slowly downwards. He smiled. 'You won't use that, you're bluffing.'

Molly poked the blade sharply forward, jabbing the Driver's hand, drawing blood.

'Ow!' the Driver yelped, recoiling.

'Right now! Open—! The—! Door—!'

The Driver sucked at his wounded hand and glared at her with murderous fury. He stepped back into his compartment; with a sigh the door folded open.

'Tickets please.'

The Conductor was four steps from the bottom; Molly sprinted for the open door, past the Driver, and leapt into the empty street.

~Chapter Ten~

Molly's feet hurt and her stomach grumbled in protest every few seconds at the continued lack of food. She wasn't sure how long she'd been walking; it must have been hours. Hours and hours and hours, though the light showed no sign of dimming to suggest the evening was approaching. She'd wandered this way and that, up and down unfamiliar streets, taking turns into yet more unfamiliar streets as the fancy took her. She may not have known every nook, cranny, and cul-de-sac of her hometown, but she was certain she would have recognised something by now; this seemingly endless parade of unfamiliar streets just wasn't possible.

After yet more aimless wandering, without passing another soul, or even hearing the sound of distant traffic, Molly decided that she would very likely die of thirst and hunger unless she took some drastic action. The next shop she passed was a small newsagent's. She tried the door, but like every other door she had tried since the Boy's house, it was locked.

'Right then,' said Molly to gee herself up, and she picked up the largest rock she could find. It was the size of a baby's head, and with careful aim she launched it through the bottom panel of glass in the shop's door. The glass shattered with an almighty crash, Molly instinctively dashing behind a hedge in case someone angry came running. She stayed put for several minutes, ears straining, stealing the odd furtive glance, before it became clear that no one was coming to investigate.

Carefully, she ducked low and shuffled through the opening she'd made, being sure to avoid the shards of glass that remained in the frame like jagged, see-through monster teeth. With her feet crunching on glass splinters, Molly stood and took in her surroundings: a normal newsagent's. She made directly for the counter first, feeling a slight thrill as she made her way behind. She quickly saw what she was looking for, and grabbed a few large plastic bags, but then tossed those aside when she spotted a large shoulder bag, presumably used by the shop's paperboy. Next she went up and down the aisles, grabbing bags of crisps, packets of biscuits and chocolate, and placing them in the paper-boy's bag. Finally she raided the tall drinks fridges, grabbing a bottle of cola and one of water too.

When the bag was too heavy to add any more, Molly slid it through the door, then ducked and shuffled after it. Once outside again she heaved the bag's strap over her neck and made her escape. Just because she hadn't seen anyone in hours, and no one had come to investigate the window smash, didn't mean it was automatically safe to stay in the shop and consume the stolen goods there. Once she was far enough away, and had taken a left and a right and a left again, she finally stopped by a tall wooden fence, slid down it onto her bum on the pavement, and delved into the bag, stuffing food hungrily into her eager mouth and washing it down with pop.

After she had consumed enough to make herself feel not only full but sick as well, Molly stopped and began to think again about her situation. About her Mum. About the monsters who had her who pretended to be the Fisks. The nice, harmless, boring old wrinkly Fisks. To her surprise she realised she had started to cry, and she rubbed the hot tears off her cheeks angrily with her sleeve.

'You are crying.'

Molly yelped in surprise. Falling to one side and leaning on her hand she looked up to see the source; it was the unnaturally Tall Man dressed all in black.

At this distance it was quickly apparent that his unusual height was far from the strangest thing about him; not only did he have not a single hair on his head, but he also didn't have any ears. Or eyes. Or nose. Just a far too large mouth.

'What? What did you say?' Molly stammered.

'Tears. Tears are what happens when a person cries. So you are crying,' the Tall Man said, matter of factly.

'Yeah? So? I'm crying, big woop!' Molly shouted at the strange man. 'So what now, hey? You've caught me at last, what are you going to do about it?' Molly found that she was too angry and bewildered to be frightened.

'Why are you crying?'

'Because... because I shouldn't be here! And I ignored everything my Gran said, or her ghost said anyway, and I'm completely lost and now the Fisks have probably put my Mum in their garden and she's dead and they're eating her soul and it's all my stupid fault! Is that enough reason for you?!' Molly realised she was up on her feet now, and had been prodding the Tall Man in the stomach angrily with her finger; not that he reacted or seemed to notice even.

'I see,' replied the Tall Man.

'Well?' said Molly.

'I am well, yes,' replied the Tall Man.

'Not 'are you well', 'what now' well?'

'You spoke to the Boy. The Boy in the room.'

'Yeah, so?'

'What did you talk about?'

'He wanted me to let him out, said he was trapped, but I think he was trying to trick me. There was blood. A lot of blood.'

'Yes. He is a very naughty Boy.'

Molly laughed at this, taking herself by surprise at its sudden eruption.

'You did well not to let him out. He would probably have torn you to pieces. You would not have enjoyed that,' said the Tall Man.

'I suppose not. It's the kind of thing that would really ruin your day, being torn to bits and your blood being splattered everywhere,' said Molly, trying to suppress the giggles again.

'I agree.'

Molly peered at the Tall Man's face, or what he had of a face. 'How can you see?'

'I can see.'

'But you don't have any eyes.'

'I can see,' said the Tall Man again.

'Okay, well that clears that up,' said Molly sarcastically, 'So can I just be clear, are you planning on doing anything horrible and painful to me?'

'No,' he replied.

'Right then. Good.' Molly slumped back onto her bum on the pavement. The Tall Man didn't move.

'You wish to help your Mother.'

'Of course I do. Stupid question.'

'Where is your Father?' The Tall Man tilted his head to one side as he asked.

'I don't....' Molly gulped back the hot prickle of tears. 'He's dead, so.'

'That is....' The Tall Man stopped as he tried to find the appropriate word, 'Sad.'

'Well, it's not happy.' Molly busied herself looking through the remnants of her snack haul. 'I didn't really know him much anyway; I was too little when he died. Barely remember him.'

'But you feel the absence.'

Molly stopped rummaging and looked up at the Tall Man, his 'face' looking blankly back. 'Yes.' She looked back down quickly. 'He was a Policeman. He helped people in trouble. Mum always says he was very good and very brave. Funny, too. Though I'm not too sure about that one.'

'And your Grandmother. The old woman in the house. She is also dead. A ghost. She also left you.'

'She was old. She got sick. She died. She tried her best not to. I didn't think it could beat her, but it did.' Molly shrugged and kept her eyes on the ground.

'Your Father and your Grandmother. And ... and another?'

Molly wondered what he meant, then she remembered, 'Neil. He was my friend. Is my friend. Was. The Fisks took him, too. He's in their garden now.'

'So many losses for one so small,' said the Tall

Man.

'Maybe I should change my name to Lucky,' said Molly; her mouth smiled, but her eyes didn't.

'That does not seem an appropriate name.'

'Yeah, that's sort of the joke.'

The Tall Man nodded, then moved his lips as though he was speaking, but no words came out.

'What? What are you saying?' said Molly.

'Go to your Mother,' said the Tall Man.

'I can't,' Molly snapped. 'I don't know where I am-!' But the Tall Man had gone. She stood and blinked dumbly in surprise. She twirled round, but he was nowhere in sight. There was no way he could have escaped from view that quickly, that was impossible.

'Well, bye then! Just leave me here, I'll be alright, I don't need your stupid help anyway!'

And that's when she saw the tree.

It was tall and wide and twisted in the middle, like someone had called its name and it was looking over its shoulder. She knew that tree. She'd fallen out of that tree last year when she and Neil were daring each other to see who could climb the highest. She'd broken her wrist when she hit the ground; she could still hear the crunching sound her bones had made as she hit the pavement. Neil had screamed and run away. It was the tree at the end of her street.

Molly whooped with joy and punched the air. Leaving the paperboy satchel behind on the ground, she sprinted down the street, towards the Fisk's, towards the monster house, towards her Mum.

~Chapter Eleven~

Molly glanced up as she passed the Boy's house; she saw him framed in the upstairs window, glaring down at her furiously, arms crossed. He stuck his tongue out; Molly returned the favour. There was no sign of Gran in the window of her own house; who knows what she must be thinking had happened to Molly.

She reached the Fisks' front gate. It was four times the size she remembered it, like it had reared up to make itself look big and scary as she approached. Molly took a few steps back; the gate was suddenly its normal size again, waist high, wooden, painted red. She shuffled forward; the gate grew, towering over her. A good trick, but Molly was pretty sure that was all it was, just some visual ju-ju to put off nosey passers-by.

'Okay then,' said Molly aloud, mentally preparing herself for whatever she was walking into. 'Here goes something....' She stood on tiptoes to reach up and pull the handle down, before leaning against the gate with her shoulder and pushing. Slowly the gate began to move under her weight, before suddenly swinging back, causing Molly to yelp and tumble to the ground.

'Ouch.' Molly got back to her feet, rubbing at her scraped elbow, and looked around; it was like night had suddenly fallen inside the Fisks' garden. Molly blinked several times to try and get her eyes used to the gloom. Over her shoulder, through the open gate, it was still light outside, but in here, within the gardens confines, it was the blackest of nights. 'Yeah, nothing weird about any of that.'

Molly moved forward cautiously. The ground beneath her feet was covered in vegetation, the crackle of twigs breaking underfoot greeting each carefully placed step. The Fisks' garden was much more than a garden; it was a forest. Giant trees towered overhead and blocked out the sun with their thick canopy. Dotted around these giant trees were smaller trees. Almost trees. Not quite trees. They looked more like trees crossed with people.

Molly looked closer.

No, not crossed with people, they <u>were</u> people;

they were all the people the Fisks had stolen over the years, all the children. Molly felt her stomach turn.

The people were stuck in the soil up to where their knees might be, their skin now bark-like: thick, coarse and cracking apart. Their arms jutted out like branches at painful angles, and their faces were partially covered by twigs, leaves, and bark outcrops from their skin. The person tree closest to Molly looked like it was probably a boy, perhaps around 9 years of age. His mouth was open as though in a silent scream, jaw trembling. His eyes were also wide; unblinking, though they twitched ever so slightly.

Back and forth.

Back and forth.

Just a millimetre or two one way, then back again. Over and over. Although the eyes were wide and bright, Molly was sure the boy wasn't actually seeing anything. Whatever he was looking at, if it was anything at all, it was not in this garden.

Molly moved a step closer to the boy planted in the soil in front of her, 'Hello? Hello, can you hear me?' The boy said nothing. Molly waved a hand back and forth in front of his restless, unseeing eyes; they gave no indication that they saw her hand.

'Somebody's in the garden

                        ...somebody...

        ...somebody...

                                ...somebody's in

the garden...'

Molly whirled as the whispered voices whisked around her from every direction, pulling the Conductor's rusty bayonet from her belt and brandishing it. 'Who is that? Come out here you coward!' But the voices fell silent again. 'Oi, do you hear me? Hiding in the trees and the dark are you? Why don't you come out and say hello?'

Molly at once felt brave and very, very hopeful that nothing would step out of the gloom to meet her challenge.

The voices remained silent; nothing stepped forward.

'Yeah, okay, that's what I thought.' She tucked the bayonet back into her belt.

Molly turned to where the Fisks' house must be, though she couldn't see it in the dark and the crush of trees. 'Best foot forward,' that's what her Gran would say. Deep breath, and forward she walked.

It was after what must have been five full minutes had passed that Molly realised the front gate wasn't the only thing about the garden that had grown. The distance from gate to front door must now be almost a mile, rather than the usual eight or nine steps. She had tried not to look too closely at the tree people that loomed all around her; she was terrified she would see one and realise it was her Mum, knee deep in the soil, eyes vacantly twitching, gone forever. Molly was so caught up in her thoughts about her Mum and the impossible garden that it took her a couple of seconds to register the hand around her wrist.

The hand grasping her was small and rough, like someone had fashioned it from ancient bark. It scratched at her as she tried to pull free. She turned to see the owner of the hand; it was a boy. He looked quite young, but in the condition he was in it was difficult to guess an age. His face was mostly obscured, lost in the unnatural vegetation sprouting from him, but she could see his mouth flapping. The jaw moving up and down as though trying desperately to speak.

'Hello?' said Molly. 'Hey, can you see me? Are you alive?'

Molly could see an eye now, it moved, bit by bit, until it was looking directly at her.

'...A...A...Andrew...' the voice rasped with difficulty, painfully dragging itself up the boy's throat and out of his mouth.

'Andrew? Is that your name?'

'He was... spoke to... me. So many... teeth and... I lost my... spoke to me...slipper. I lost my...'

Molly gasped. The slipper! A single slipper had been all that was found, the only evidence left behind. 'Billy? Billy Tyler, is that you?'

'Lost my slipper,' said what had become of poor Billy Tyler, 'Spoke to... maths tomorrow...Andrew.' The wooden hand loosened its grip on Molly's wrist as Billy Tyler raised his arm into the air. The arm cracked hideously as it bent backwards against the elbow and settled into its parody of a twisted tree branch. Billy Tyler's mouth no longer flapped and his eye no longer looked at Molly or registered anything at all.

'Billy? Billy, can you hear me? Billy!' But Billy Tyler said nothing and saw nothing and thought nothing.

This would not happen to her Mum. What they had done to Billy Tyler, to everyone in this garden, to Neil, it would not happen to her Mum. She would not allow it. She turned back to the Fisks' house and ran, ran past more of the planted people with their wide unseeing eyes and twisted limbs. How many had the Fisks taken? How many had they feasted upon? For how many years had they hidden in plain sight stealing people away? Molly ran and she ran, until finally the Fisks' house was revealed, emerging from the dark suddenly like a trapdoor spider from its hiding place.

She looked down at the mat beneath her feet; the word 'Welcome' was stitched across it. She had never thought a welcome mat to be sinister before.

Molly was relieved to see that the house didn't share the garden's giant proportions; it looked just like it did in the real Awake world. Same bricks, same front door, same windows, same size. Time for check one. She knelt by the letterbox, slowly pulling the outer flap open with one hand whilst pushing the inner flap open with the other, and then peering inside. An empty corridor. She put her ear to it, straining to try and hear anything at all. Silence.

Next she half shuffled, half waddled in a crouched position over to the front room's window, grasping the bottom of the wooden frame and lifting her head above it just enough to see inside. The thick curtains were wide open; the room beyond was empty.

Okay, that was check number two; the next one was high risk but she needed to know if the Fisks were inside and she could think of no other way. She stood before the front door, lifted a finger, counted silently to three, and pressed the doorbell. As she turned and raced towards a tree to hide, she heard the Fisks' doorbell sounding out a chirpy, jolly tune. Molly waited, stealing glances at the windows to try and spy any sign of movement, even the twitch of a curtain, but there was nothing. No one answered the door. The house was unoccupied.

'Right,' said Molly. 'Right then. Okay. I can do this. I am doing this. Because I'm brave and I'm tough and no stupid monsters are going to scare me.' Molly thought of Mr Adams, *'I'll grab hold of old Mr Death and give him what for! Front line, girl. Front line.'*

'Only way to live.'

Molly swallowed once and marched boldly back to the front door. She pushed the handle down expecting it to be locked. The door swung open, causing Molly to almost fall flat on her face in surprise. She regained her balance and looked around self-consciously, but of course there was no one to see her almost face-plant but a garden full of unseeing dead tree children.

She was inside. She was in the Fisks' house Between. Now she just had to hope Mum was still in here, and not out there. She shook her head to get rid of any such thoughts; Mum was not in the garden, she hadn't been planted in the soil, not like Billy Tyler— Mum was in this house somewhere, she just knew it. She had to be.

Molly stepped forward.

The house smelled of old tobacco, of air freshener, and something else. What was that 'something else'? Under the tobacco and air freshener, a staleness. A dankness. Like the mould that grows on the walls in basements. She walked carefully towards the first door; it was already half open and lead into the front room. Stepping inside, she could see framed photographs of the Fisks on the walls, smiling. The same Fisks she'd seen every day for the last eight years, the same Fisks she'd spoken to more times than she could remember, the same Fisks who had happily nattered away to her about gardening and the old days and what the street had been like years ago. They liked to point out houses to Molly and tell her who had lived there before, the other residents of her street who had come and gone whilst the Fisks remained, twinkly eyed, laughing, pruning their plants. Looking after Jeff the Bush.

She turned to leave when she spotted something;

it was a small plant pot on the coffee table. What was that sticking up out of the soil? Three twigs from a tree? Molly looked closer: no, not three twigs, three fingers. Three small fingers, skin turned to bark like the planted people outside, ragged fingernails visible at the top of each. Molly remembered the Fisks taking cuttings to plant inside from 'Cathy' days earlier. Brighten up the front room, they'd said. Molly shuddered.

Back into the corridor, the dank, mouldy smell grew stronger as she passed the door under the staircase; Molly made her way into the back room. More pictures, a couch, a table with a half finished jigsaw on it of one of those giant mazes made from tall hedges you get in the grounds of big fancy houses. This led through into the kitchen, the mould stench lessening as she moved further from the corridor, from the staircase, from that door.

The kitchen was as ordinary as they come. Or at least it would have been thirty years ago, such was the age of the garish units and old-fashioned lino flooring that peeled upwards in the corners. Molly pulled at the fridge door, the light inside came on, and what she saw made her immediately regret the decision. A head. It looked back at her, eyes turned dry and yellow in their sockets. Molly slammed the fridge door shut and walked quickly back out, through the back room and into the corridor again, hand over her mouth.

The door under the stairs was there, waiting. The

smell of mould and of festering decay seeping from behind it to envelop her. Molly could have gone upstairs, checked the bedrooms, the bathroom, the attic, but she knew. She knew if her Mum was anywhere inside this house, it was behind that door.

She wrapped her fingers around the brass knob; it was cold and sticky to the touch. Tacky, unclean. She turned it; the scraping complaint seemed almost like that of an animal, not old, rusty metal. She pulled the door forward and staggered backwards as the smell assaulted her, causing her to turn and almost vomit up the unhealthy feast she'd wolfed down earlier. The smell was almost visible, rolling lazily out of the darkened doorway. Molly caught her breath, blocked her nose, and then stepped inside.

It was pitch black within; she felt around on the wall for a light switch. The wall was warm, damp, and soft beneath her wandering fingers. Finally she found the switch and pressed it. There was a second or two's delay before the spluttering flicker of bare bulbs cast a low light, just enough to see. She peered at the soft wall; it seemed a dark red under this poor lighting. Not red-red, not strawberry red, more a sort of dull, fleshy red, like raw meat. She touched it again and gasped as the wall seemed to writhe beneath her hand, like it was alive, like it was a creature responding to her touch.

In front of her a wooden staircase led downwards. Molly took each step carefully, trying not to touch the flesh walls which continued to move and twitch and judder. This was no ordinary basement; it was like she was actually inside a living beast, like Jonah in the belly of the whale.

Even with the lights on, the illumination cast was too weak to be able to make out much; most of the room remained hidden in shadow. Even so, Molly could see the space wasn't empty; large darkened piles surrounded her. She approached the nearest pile; it was soil.

She moved to the next, more soil, and onto the next. Molly's heart jumped into her mouth, something was on the soil. No, not something. Someone. 'Mum!' Molly shouted joyfully. She wasn't too late! The Fisks hadn't put her in the garden yet!

Molly raced over to her; Mum was curled up on her side like she was asleep in her bed. Yes, that was all, just asleep. Molly could feel her breathing as she hugged her tightly.

Mum stirred slightly in her arms. 'Molly...?' she said, still half asleep.

'We've got to go right now!' Molly shook her. 'Mum, come on, wake up; please!'

Mum opened her eyes full and tried to focus on Molly, eyes bleary, 'Oh; hello Moll's. I was having just the weirdest dream. Your Dad was there, I think. All dressed up in his Police uniform. Only no, no it wasn't him, not when I stepped outside, then he had these teeth, these sharp teeth—'

'Okay, good, I really want to hear that, but let's get out of here first, yes?'

'What time is it? Have you had breakfast?' Her Mum sat up, stretching. 'Eww, what is that smell?' She still seemed dazed, not completely aware as she looked around, trying to focus in the basement's gloom. 'Where are we?'

'At the Fisks', come on, let's get home, now.' Molly pulled at her arm and her Mum staggered up, feet slipping in the soil. As they reached the stairs, Mum reached out a hand to steady herself, touching the fleshy wall.

'That's not stone, that's... is that alive?'

'Come on, Mum! We don't have time for this now!' Molly snapped, pulling her Mum desperately forwards.

'Oh, I'm still asleep, aren't I? This is where I was in the dream you see, in the flesh room. The stinky old flesh room. Such a weird dream, but so sort of real, too.'

'Mum! Come on!' screamed Molly.

'Okay, okay, I'm coming, there's no need to shout. You know if this wasn't a dream I'd give you a right telling of for talking to me like that.' And Mum laughed as the flesh walls seemed to breathe in and out in a panic.

She laughed a little less when the room began to scream.

~Chapter Twelve~

Molly and her Mum ran into the garden full of planted people as the basement continued to scream in outrage behind them. Scream at the thief who stole away the garden's latest addition, scream a warning to the Fisks that someone had trespassed into their inner sanctum.

'Oh!' said Mum as they raced past the gardens ghoulish exhibits, their limbs twisted and bent at unnatural angles. 'I remember this place, sort of; it's horrible. Was I eating cheese before bed? That's probably it. You should never eat cheese before bed, you know Molly. Gives you the loopiest dreams, but people plants?'

'Okay then, no cheese before bed, got it!'

'Or trees, they're more like trees really aren't they? Well, that's a new one on me!' And Mum laughed and laughed as Molly kept pulling her forward towards the front gate.

'Look at the size of that gate!' said Mum. 'Why would I dream a massive gate?!'

At every step Molly looked for any signs of the Fisks return, expecting them to emerge from the undergrowth at any moment.

But they didn't appear, and soon enough they out they were out of the garden, into the street beyond and past the Boy's house. 'You can tell this is a dream,' said Mum, 'because even though this is our street, it's not quite right is it? That front door over there's the wrong colour for a start, and that house is supposed to have a tree in the front garden, not potted plants!'

Soon they were back in their own home; Molly slammed the door shut and locked it.

'You know I'm very tired all of a sudden, it's strange to be tired in a dream, isn't it?' said Mum. 'I think I might go up to bed. Up to bed in a dream to sleep in a dream.' And with that she headed upstairs to her room, chuckling and shaking her head.

Molly leant back against the locked front door and finally allowed herself to feel the relief. She'd done it; she'd rescued her Mum and hadn't even had to face off against the Fisks. After a few moments she bounded up the staircase and peeped through the small crack in the doorway into her Mum's room; she was curled up under the covers. As she fell to sleep she began to fade away, until finally the bed was empty.

Molly ran in and threw the covers back, but there was no one there.

'Mum!'

'It's okay, Molly, she's Awake now.' Molly turned to see her Gran in the doorway.

'She's safe? She's back home?'

'Well, she's back home, yes.'

Molly ran to her dead Gran and hugged her tightly. 'I did it.' Gran held her and stroked her hair gently.

'Yes, you did. Nothing and no one gets in the way of my Molly Brown.'

'You will not believe what happened to me,' Molly said. 'There was this boy who I think might have been some sort of monster, and then there was this bus full of corpses and a zombie murder conductor guy, and the Tall Man without a face who was following me. I thought I was never going to get back.'

'I told you, Molly, you cannot trust the Between; it changes, moves, deceives. You could have been lost out there forever,' said Gran, a hint of annoyance in her voice to let Molly know she meant business, that Molly should have listened to her and not let herself be distracted.

'Sorry, but everything went okay in the end. I got

Mum back from that house; she isn't in the garden with Billy Tyler and the rest. I showed those stupid old Fisks not to mess with me.'

'Oh, yes you did.'

'Will I see you again?' asked Molly, looking up into her Gran's grey face.

'You can come here any time you like now that you've been here once. You just need to go to sleep thinking of here, and if you do you'll slip Between. Any time you do, I will know, and I'll be here.'

They walked back to Gran's room, arm in arm, and sat side by side on the bed. Molly told her all about the adventure she'd been on, about the Conductor's attack and the bloody handprints and Billy Tyler in the garden and of the flesh basement that screamed. When she finally stopped her excited gabbling, Gran smiled and ruffled her hair.

'The Fisks know,' said Gran.

'That I've got Mum out?'

'Yes, I can feel it. The basement called out to them when you were escaping. Wherever they were, the Fisks will have heard it, too,' said Gran.

'It's alive, the house, isn't it?'

'In a way it is, yes.'

'They'll be angry, I expect; monsters don't like their food being stolen. I'm not a monster and even I hate that,' said Molly.

Gran laughed, 'Yes. Which means you no longer have the luxury of trying to talk your Mum into moving away, though I don't expect that would have really worked in the first place. The Fisks will come for both of you now; you trespassed on their home Between, stole from them, saw their secrets. They won't let that pass.'

'What now then? What can we do?' asked Molly.

Gran smiled. 'Now, Molly dear? Well, now we fight!'

~Chapter Thirteen~

Molly awoke with a start, sitting bolt upright on her Gran's bed. She looked at the bedside clock. It was just a normal clock again, with the ordinary, normal number of hands; she was back in the real world. She was Awake again. What's more, it seemed like hardly any time had passed; it was still bright and early in the morning, not even nine o'clock. A muffled clatter alerted her to the fact that someone was bashing around in the kitchen. Molly jumped to her feet and rushed downstairs. In the kitchen her Mum was making a cooked breakfast; bacon sizzled in the pan, eggs ready to fry nearby.

'Hey Molls, how much bacon d'you want? I'm starving!' Molly grinned and ran at her Mum, hugging her tightly, her Mum looking down in surprise. 'Woah! What have I done to deserve this?'

'You didn't get eaten,' said Molly.

'Oh. Okay. Bit of a weird answer.' And Mum ruffled Molly's messy hair affectionately before turning back to the bacon. 'You know I had such a weird dream. You were in it actually.'

'Oh really?' said Molly, smiling.

'I was in the Fisks basement, only it was alive and they were going to plant me in their garden, like all those plants they're always doting over. Only instead of just being nice and watering and pruning me, they would eat me. Or eat my soul. Something like that. I'll have to tell them about it, I bet they'll find it a hoot,' said Mum.

'No!' shouted Molly firmly.

Mum looked at Molly in blank surprise. 'Excuse me?'

'I mean, why go near the Fisks at all? They're so sort of boring and dull and they really smell.'

'They smell,' said Mum, unimpressed.

'Yes! You must have noticed.'

'Smell of what?' asked Mum.

'Oh, just, you know... stuff. Smelly stuff,' said Molly sheepishly.

'Now you just stop that. The Fisks might be more than a touch on the dull side, but they're a nice old couple and you will not talk about them like that,' said Mum, giving her best stern glare, before breaking into a smile. 'Though yes, I suppose they are a bit smelly. Poor pair.' Mum and Molly laughed as the doorbell rang.

'Go and get that will you Molls? I'll crack the eggs.'

Molly sighed and went to answer the door as the bell rang out again. 'Okay, okay, I'm coming!' she yelled, annoyed, pulling the door wide to reveal two familiar, crinkly faces smiling sweetly back. It was the Fisks.

Molly froze as she looked back and forth at the pair, they no longer looked like harmless old Mr and Mrs Fisk— or actually they did, but now that she looked at them she could see these two old people for the disguise they were. She could feel the coiled danger beneath the sagging skin, see the malevolence slithering in their watery eyes.

'Well, well and I never did or could; look who it is Mr Fisk, look who it really and actually in all honesty is.' A dry tongue darted from between thin, peeling lips, licking, hungry.

'Is it? Could it be or do my ancient yellowed eyes deceive me? Is it Molly, dear? We really did wonder what could have become of you, it's been such a time since we laid our old eyes on you last.'

'Go away,' Molly hissed.

'Goes away? Is that what she said to her dear old friends and neighbours? Friends who taught her how to keep a tidy, colourful, bountiful garden? Who pointed at all the plants and told her their real and actually truthful names?'

'What could have brought on such a hurtful outcry I must ask myself in indignation?'

'Who is it?' asked Mum from the kitchen.

'No one! Wrong house!' shouted Molly, trying to throw the door closed, but a wrinkled, bony, claw of a hand, fingernails long and ragged, grasped the edge and pushed forward with surprising force, sending Molly tumbling backwards onto the floor.

'It's us, Mrs Brown! Your favourite neighbours who ain't in fact Mr Adams the ex-military man.'

'Mrs Fisk?' shouted Mum, 'Come through, the kettle's just boiled.'

Molly went to kick the door shut on them, but before she could even raise her leg the Fisks had moved with a speed she would never think their withered old bodies capable of and were already disappearing through the kitchen door.

'Crap it—' Molly leapt up and dashed into the kitchen, where Mr Fisk was already slurping hot tea, his eyes narrow and amused as he peered at her from over the rim of his mug.

'You would not and never could believe the horrors myself and my good sound husband of many years here have most recently endured, Mrs Brown,' said Mrs Fisk, mock indignant.

'Oh? What's happened? Not that dog from number eleven leaving its mess on your lawn again?' asked Mum.

Mr Fisk snorted. 'No, not that yappy little fiend, we already done for him, dealt with him we have, we deals with things you see.' Mr Fisk's eyes met Molly's again as he finished his sentence.

'We had what you might say was very much an unwanted and illegal intruder!'

'No! A break-in? Are you okay?' asked Mum.

'Oh, I am, made of sterner stuff than most I am, ain't I?' crowed Mr Fisk, 'But it has put the wind up something terrible for my lovely lady wife here. Not safe in your own home anymore! People come in, uninvited, don't they?'

'Got home we did, me and Mr Fisk, to find the front door wide, muddy prints up and down the carpet, something that was ours, our very own, ripped and taken from the premises. From our very own and private basement even! Something we deserves and wishes so very much that we had back.'

'Will have back,' Mr Fisk interjected.

Mrs Fisk nodded with enthusiasm. 'All being well and good, Mr Fisk, oh yes....'

Molly stood straight and defiant under their glaring eyes.

'That is just awful,' said Mum.

'Maybe they, whoever it was that broke in, was taking something back that wasn't yours anyway. Maybe you deserved it!' Molly stepped back, surprised at the strength of her outburst. She looked to her Mum, who was starring at her, eyes wide and dumbfounded.

'Molly, what on Earth would make you say such a horrible thing!' said Mum. 'Apologise right this second!'

'No I won't! I will not apologise to them; you don't know what they really are!' Molly was pointing at the Fisks, who were almost unable to stop themselves from sniggering. Molly knew there was no way to explain things, to make Mum believe her. It was crazy; who would believe it?

'I'm going to have to ask you to ignore my daughter. I don't know what's got into her today.'

'That's okay, Mrs Brown, we know the ways of the young and spirited and ripe for the picking, their emotions do bubble up and spill out unbidden at times, you can't and really shouldn't hold it against the poor mites,' said Mrs Fisk.

'That's very understanding, Mrs Fisk, but I won't stand for it. Molly, get to your room, now.'

Mum glared at Molly, but she stood firm.

'No, I won't go,' Molly replied.

Mum blinked dumbly twice. 'I beg your pardon young lady?'

'Not until they've gone; not until they're out of our house.' Molly crossed her arms and planted her feet wide to show she meant it.

'I'm so sorry, Mr and Mrs Fisk—'

'Oh no, no need, we knows where we isn't wanted or needed or desired; off we pop Mr Fisk.'

'Yes, yes, back to our broken cold home to lick our poor wounds and wonder who next might break our homes safety and avail their hands of what's ours.'

Molly stepped back as Mr and Mrs Fisk made for the front door, Mr Fisk turning to look at Molly, his eyes slithering over her, making her feel as though they actually left a greasy streak on her skin. 'See you soon, Molly girl. Yes, yes. Believe that.' And then they were gone and the front door was heard to open and close.

Molly exhaled with relief, sagging slightly. She looked up to her Mum, who, it appeared, didn't know whether to be furious or gobsmacked and so was wavering somewhere in between. 'Well? What in Heaven's name was all that about?'

'Trust me, Mum, we don't want those two in our house ever again. I'll go to my room now.' Molly turned and headed towards the stairs, leaving her Mum to finally commit to being fully gobsmacked.

~Chapter Fourteen~

Molly had a plan. In the Between she and her dead Gran had spoken about what needed to be done. There were no two ways about it; the Fisks needed to be got gone. They had hidden for centuries, according to Gran. Countless people had been dragged from their half-slumber and planted in the garden, to be feasted upon by the Fisks' monstrous real selves that they hid in the safety of the Between. Well, no more; their stone had been upturned, but rather than scuttle away like a beetle startled by its sudden reveal, the Fisks would fight, and if they were given the chance to fight, they would win.

Molly had to take the fight to them; it was the last

thing two such as the Fisks would expect, so certain and comfortable were they in the belief that they were untouchable. Gran couldn't do much but offer advice and moral support, limited as she was to the four walls of the house, but that didn't mean she was going to let her Granddaughter tackle the monsters alone. Molly would need help, and Gran knew just the man for the job.

Time was of the essence; the Fisks wouldn't allow anything perceived as a threat to run free for long so Molly wanted to get right to it. Unfortunately, after her outburst in the kitchen, Mum wasn't going to let Molly go anywhere.

'But I just need to do something; it'll take a minute and I'll be right back, promise!' pleaded Molly.

'Not a chance, young lady, now you just get back up to your room and stay there,' replied an unimpressed Mum, arms crossed.

Molly sat on her bed, leg jiggling in worry. She ran over to the bedroom window and peered out; but it was no good. No tree near enough to help her clamber out, no drainpipe within reach to shimmy down, and she didn't fancy her ankles' chances if she tried to dangle out and drop to the ground below.

So she waited.

This was a risk, she knew that. Who was to say that when her Mum went to sleep the Fisks wouldn't be waiting for that moment when she was between awake and asleep to grab hold of her and pull her back into their world? So, after hours and hours, when her Mum finally went up to bed, Molly crept up the landing to lurk outside her bedroom door. Luckily Mum had something of a fear of the dark so always slept with the door partially open and the landing light on. Molly stood silently, watching over the shape of her Mum in bed, ready to rush in to shake her awake at the first hint of her starting to fade away to nothing.

Once Mum was properly, fully asleep, she would be safe; she would have moved past the point where she was vulnerable, and at that point, if they got to that point, Molly could slip out and go for help.

Mum tossed and turned, before finally getting up to head downstairs for a glass of water, causing Molly to scuttle quickly back into her own room. After Mum didn't appear again for almost ten minutes, Molly shuffled out and stood on the landing, straining to hear the sound of her Mum moving around, or of the TV blaring late night programmes; but nothing. Silence.

Molly panicked, running down the stairs three steps at a time, dashing around the ground floor. Was she too late? What if her Mum had fallen asleep down here and the Fisks already had her? There was no way they'd hold onto her in the basement like last time; she'd be straight into the soil, planted in their garden as soon as they had their yellowed hands on her and it would be all Molly's fault for taking her eyes off her.

Molly's heart was beating as though it might burst from her chest, when a soft snuffle caught her ear from the couch, and there she was. Mum, curled up, half drunk glass of water on the floor, fast asleep.

'Mum?' said Molly quietly, then louder. 'Hey, Mum.' She didn't even stir. The Fisks hadn't taken her; she was past the in-between phase and in a deep sleep. She was safe, for now. Molly smiled and gently placed a kiss onto her sleeping Mum's head, before heading for the front door, and, as quietly as she could manage, opening it, slipping outside, and closing it again behind her.

She shivered in the sudden cold of the night air, hugging herself and rubbing her sides with her hands to try and warm herself up. She was dressed only in her thin pyjamas; in her rush it hadn't crossed her mind to put her coat on. Oh well, there was no time to lose, no going back.

To her right light filtered through thick curtains from an upstairs window at the Fisk's house. She looked at the garden, which looked just as it always had done. Normal lawn, flowerbeds and plants, tended to with pride, but Molly knew the truth. Billy Tyler was in there, half-dead, half-alive, a grotesque parody forever lost. Had he recognised her when he reached out? Was he aware of what he was doing, what he'd been trying to say, or was it a reflex memory? Was the real him still alive in there, terrified, in pain, in horror at what had become of him? Molly shivered again, but this time it was nothing to do with the cold.

***

Mr Adams was asleep in his favourite comfy chair, the material on the arms worn and frayed from years of use. His chin was down on his chest, eyes closed, pictures from the muted television set flickering as they projected onto his skin. Books packed the shelves in an untidy fashion, as well as in piles scattered higgledy-piggledy around the room on the thick, brown carpet. Most were about the army, about adventurers, about the unknown. About great battles fought and won, or fought and lost; grand, brave men doing what they thought was right.

Over the fireplace, dominating the room, was a large framed picture of a British Army battalion, lines of stiffly stood young men with stern, proud faces; and in there, second row, fourth from the right, was a twenty two year old Mr Adams. Young, fit, with his whole life of proud adventure in front of him.

Mr Adams shifted in his chair as memories washed over him. Years of life splashing against each other, creating adventures anew for the snoozing Mr Adams, young again as he grasped a pistol and ran headlong towards the screams for help with no thought for his own safety, only of doing the right thing.

The doorbell rang.

Mr Adams heard it distantly, but now he was taking tea with Yeti and it would be rude to leave them; goodness knows what a fully grown Yeti would do to an Englishman who disrespected him!

The doorbell again, accompanied this time by a hand knocking at the window.

'Mr Adams!'

Mr Adams opened his eyes and looked blearily around, wondering what had happened to the mountains, to the monsters, before remembering that all of that was done and gone. Long ago finished. He lived in this house now, surrounded by memories, body old and past its best. The doorbell rang again, and again.

'Now, now, I hear you! Wait a minute, won't you?' said Mr Adams, mouth dry. With a groan he eased himself up out of his chair and onto his feet. He smoothed down the lines of his clothes and walked crisply towards whoever was calling at this ruddy late of an hour. He threw open the front door, ready to give whatever bounder stood behind it a damn good talking to, only to find any outburst forgotten as he saw Molly Brown stood on his doorstep, shivering and hugging herself, her eyes wide and worried. 'Now, Molly girl, what's all this, then? It's late, you know, you should be tuckered out and tucked up.'

'Mr Adams, you're the only one that can help,' said Molly, teeth chattering.

'Help, is it? What d'you mean?'

'Monsters, Mr Adams; we have monsters to fight.'

~Chapter Fifteen~

Molly sat on the plump couch, a thick, warm blanket that Mr Adams had given her wrapped around her body twice. She'd never actually been inside Mr Adams's house before, it wasn't as tidy as she had expected; in fact, it was a complete and total tip. Masses of books piled all around, and yellowing bundles of years-old newspapers. Plates poked out from under furniture with bread crusts turned hard and flecked with mould. Outside of the house you'd think him the most orderly man alive, but it was clear he liked to let everything hang out behind closed doors.

'Now then, here we go, young Molly girl, fresh

cup of hot tea, that'll do the job, warm you right through,' said Mr Adams as he entered the front room, kicking a pile of old newspapers out of his way and placing a tray holding two large mugs of steaming tea and a packet of digestive biscuits onto the coffee table. Molly took her mug and munched on a biscuit.

'Thanks,' she said, spraying biscuit crumbs.

'Please don't mind the unruly state of my digs; a man's home should be full and messy with life and information! Shows a busy, sharp mind, that does me girl! Also, I don't like cleaning up. Waste of time if you ask me.' Molly nodded. Mr Adams kicked another pile of newspapers aside and sat in his chair. 'Well then, Molly my girl; monsters is it?'

Molly nodded and blew on the tea to cool it.

'I see. Tricky blighters, monsters you know. And such a variety of the buggers, that's the thing; rules for one don't apply to the other, or vice versa. Did I ever tell you about the time I had tea with a family of Yeti?'

'Yes,' said Molly, chancing a mouthful of the still too hot tea.

'Ah. Yes,' said Mr Adams, looking momentarily crestfallen. 'I suppose I've told you all my stories a hundred times now. Nothing new to add to the roll for such a long time.'

'Until now,' said Molly, grinning.

'Oh yes, so you say. Monsters! Well, well. It must be very serious for you to be sneaking out of your warm home in your jim-jams at such an hour.'

'The most serious thing ever,' said Molly gravely.

'I see. Best fill me in then, yes? Give me an idea of the task we're up against.'

And so Molly told Mr Adams everything. About the Between. About the Fisks. About the people planted in their garden. About her ghost Gran. Even about the boy locked in the room, the bus, and the man without a face. Out it all blurted in one continuous stream, as Mr Adams sat nodding, taking it all in, never once interrupting.

'And so, well, then I knocked on your door and ate your biscuits,' said Molly, finally up to date.

'I see,' said Mr Adams, before slapping his knees and getting to his feet. 'Well there's no time to waste, is there, my girl? Let's show these monstrous blighters what for!'

Molly blinked once or twice in silent surprise. 'You believe me? You just believe me, no questions?'

'Shouldn't I?' asked Mr Adams in surprise.

'It's just, well, it's not a very believable story. It's a really stupid sounding story, in fact. I thought I'd have trouble convincing you.'

'You've never shown yourself to be anything but truthful far as I can see, Molly, why should you start lying to me now? No, believe me, I can sense when I'm being lied to; I can see it in a person's eyes.'

'You didn't know the Fisks had been lying.'

'Ah, now did I or did I not say 'person', hm? Monsters are not people, different set of rules altogether. Sneaky as you like, monsters; born to lie, it's inbuilt, nothing to betray them, you've got to catch them in the actual act, you know.'

'Gran said you'd believe me,' said Molly, beaming.

'Course she did, one of the wisest people I ever met, your Gran, she's no fool, she knows what's what. Fine woman. Sort of woman I would have married if I'd ever had any interest in that sort of thing.'

Molly discarded the biscuits and leapt to her feet. 'Okay then. Let's do it!'

Mr Adams smiled, 'What say you and I go bag us some monsters, hey?'

~Chapter Sixteen~

Molly left Mr Adams's house with a spring in her step. She'd found the man to help her destroy the monsters; now she needed to get back home and find her way back Between.

'Well I never did, looks who it is, Mr Fisk.' Molly froze, her heart fluttering. She turned to see the Fisks stood in their garden, eyeing her with oily malevolence as she shivered in the dark.

'Stay back!' said Molly, trying to sound firm and determined, rather than cold and scared.

'Stay back she says, to us, her old friends and neighbours who's been with her through thick and thin alike,' said Mr Fisk, mockingly.

'Was we not there with a tender word and kind eyes when your dear old Gran shuffled off her mortal coil and completely in fact died a death? Hm?'

'Don't you talk about my Gran. She was the first to see you for what you really are.'

'Was she now? Well, well I never,' said Mrs Fisk with a chuckle.

'And what exactly might we in fact be, child?' asked Mr Fisk.

'Monsters. Killers. Evil.'

Mr Fisk leant back, hand to his chest in faux-surprise. 'Cuts me to the quick does that, Molly, such vicious if not entirely untrue words dropping out from between your youngster gums.'

'We're going to stop you,' said Molly with certainty.

'We are, are we? We and Gran, is it? Or 'praps you mean silly old Mr Adams. That's where you been, is it? Recruiting?'

'We're going to stop you. Stop you hurting anyone else, stop you putting people in your sick garden.' Molly moved towards her front door, keeping her eyes fixed on the Fisks. They didn't move, quite still, quite calm, eyes not blinking even once as they remained fixed to hers. Their mouths stayed in permanent smirks, so certain were they of their power, of their superior position.

'So you thinks you might come back to our real

home and kills us stone dead, is that it girly?'

'Oh, that's exactly it,' said Molly.

'Gots to fall asleep for that; ain't that true and right, Mr Fisk?'

'True and right enough, Mrs Fisk.'

'So what's to stop the horrible old monstrous likes of us from taking you and gobbling you up as you drift between worlds, hm?'

'My Gran won't let you. She's there; she's waiting. She'll make sure I arrive Between safely.'

Mr and Mrs Fisk laughed, thick phlegm hacking up and down their throats.

'Good old Gran, she always was a strong headed one, weren't she? But don't you be worried Molly girl, we wants you to step across all safe and sound.'

'It'll be more fun and games that, way. We gets to savour the chase. So few times we really gets to savour the chase.'

Molly shivered, then silently cursed herself for showing weakness. 'It'll be me that does the chasing,' she said.

The Fisks laughed again, louder this time.

'Oh goody.'

'We've got a nice spot all ready Molly, haven't we Mr Fisk?'

'Oh yes, yes. Nice bit of fresh, nutrient-rich soil all pegged out and ready for a rare and unique flower; now what's the technical name of that rare and soon to be ours flower, wife of mine?'

Mrs Fisk's lips peeled back to reveal her yellow

and brown stained teeth. 'Molly, husband of mine. It's called Molly.'

Molly threw her front door open and jumped inside, quickly shutting out the Fisks and their dusty laughter. 'Oh no,' said Molly, 'not me. You won't get me, because I'm going to get you first.'

She checked on her Mum, still curled up asleep on the couch, snoring gently. Molly made her way upstairs to Gran's room and hopped into bed, pulling the covers tight around her. Now all she needed to do was fall asleep. Just fall asleep. Eyes shut, off to sleepy byes. Easy as that. After several futile minutes Molly sat up. Her mind was buzzing, thoughts whirling and chasing each other, heart beating like it was trying to break through her rib cage; how on Earth was she going to drift off to sleep in this state? And Mr Adams! She needed to be there to wake him otherwise he'd slip past and become fully Asleep; or worse, the Fisks might grab him.

Molly flopped back down again and kicked at the covers in frustration. What could she do? She wasn't in the least bit tired—

'Close your eyes.'

Molly blinked several times in mute surprise, 'What?'

'Close your eyes.'

'Gran? Gran is that you?' Molly wasn't hearing her Gran's voice, not exactly; more she was sensing it, bubbling up inside her brain.

'Close your eyes, Molly, and go to sleep.'

'I'm trying but I'm not at all tired,' said Molly, and she yawned. 'Oh, well, maybe I am. A bit.'

'Go to sleep now. I'm waiting for you.'

And Molly closed her heavy eyes and fell quickly to sleep.

~Chapter Seventeen~

Molly awoke Between. Her dead Gran was sat at the bottom of the bed waiting. 'Hello darling.'

Molly threw herself down the bed and hugged her Gran's grey body, 'Gran!'

'Careful, darling, I'm dead not indestructible!' said Gran.

'They know. The Fisks know and they're going to try and kill us.'

Gran stroked Molly's hair and smiled. 'Yes, I thought they would. All went well with Mr Adams?'

'He believed me straight away. I told him to wait an hour, then to go to sleep; that would give me enough time to get here and to pull him through.'

Gran released Molly from her embrace and looked her in the eyes. 'Then go, go now, you show the Fisks what you're made of.'

Molly stood and stepped towards the door, only to pause.

'I might not win. I mean, the Fisks might kill me, might put me in their garden.'

Gran smiled sadly. 'Yes. Yes they might.'

'But I have to try, don't I?'

'Is that what you think?' asked Gran.

Molly knew there was only one answer. 'It's what Dad would do. People are in danger. They have to be stopped and no one else is going to do it.'

'Braveheart, Molly,' said Gran, and though her mouth was smiling, her eyes were full of worry.

***

Molly opened the front door a crack to peer out. Just like last time the absence of noise was quite pronounced and startling. She pulled the door fully open and looked around for any sign of the Fisks laying in wait to attack her, but all seemed clear. Taking a deep breath, she stepped out of the safety of her house and into the outside world. Glancing warily around for any sign of danger, she thought she caught sight of the tall faceless man in black, but in the time it took to blink he'd gone.

Molly turned her back on the Fisks unnatural garden and ran over to the low wooden fencing that separated her own front garden from Mr Adams's. She scrabbled over, trampling on Mr Adams's flower bed, and rushed to his front door; it was open a crack.

'Mr Adams?' she called quietly. No answer. She pushed the front door open and stepped inside. It looked just as it had done in the real world, with piles of newspapers, unopened mail, and abandoned mugs each concealing half an inch of congealed black coffee.

'Mr Adams?' Molly called again, louder this time. She began to worry. Had the Fisks got to him first? The door had been open; perhaps they'd tempted him outside and all was already lost? Was he even now within their home, down in the flesh basement awaiting the soil? 'Mr Adams!'

'Who goes there? Friend or monster?' replied Mr Adams forcefully from upstairs.

Molly's heart skipped a beat as the relief washed over her. 'It's me, Mr Adams!' she shouted.

Mr Adams stepped into view at the top of the staircase, legs planted wide and firm. He was dressed like he was ready for an expedition into strange new lands un-trod by human foot, an antique rifle in hand and pointed down towards Molly. 'How do I know you're telling the truth, hm? I've come across more than one shape-shifter in my time, oh yes. Once in, I think it was Nepal, a young lady entered our camp, only after we had the common courtesy to feed and water her she changed without a moment's notice into some sort of toothy goblin chap. All green and scaly, teeth as sharp as razors.

Very nearly bit my second in command's left foot off. Chap was in quite a state after that fright, I can tell you.'

'What did you do to the goblin?'

'Hm? Oh, bashed it over the head with the pan we'd been cooking baked beans in, knocked it clean out, handed it over to the proper authorities. Now tell me, girl, are you a toothy goblin creature in disguise?'

'No, I am not; I'm Molly, your neighbour. Now how on Earth are you already here? Someone Between has to pull you in; you don't just appear here.'

Mr Adams lowered his gun, all thoughts of Molly possibly being a foot-biting goblin apparently having exited his train of thought. 'Oh, I don't need a guide anywhere, not me, not with all my accumulated years of experience, found me own way here, oh yes! Been trained by the best when it comes to trances, meditation and the art of astral projection, you know. I just put myself under and willed myself to enter what you referred to as 'The Between'. Next thing I know, I open my eyes and here I am, done up in my finest explorer togs, clearly in my house but not my house. If that makes sense.'

Molly nodded. It did not surprise her that a marvellous man such as Mr Adams, who had seen and done so many eye-widening and thrilling things during his life, would be able to find his way to a place such as this very easily and under his own steam.

There was a sharp knock at the front door.

'Who goes there!' Mr Adams raised his rifle and trained it on the door, squinting down the barrel.

'It's them, the Fisks, it must be!'

'Never fear, girl. Okay you out there, state your name and business or expect a sharp reply!' said Mr Adams as he made his way swiftly down the staircase so that he was stood facing the front door, rifle steadily trained on it, Molly to his side.

A second knock.

'Oi, he said state your name, are you deaf?' said Molly.

'You heard her, got no time for messing about, either state your business or clear off, you hear me?'

'Jack,' came a man's voice from outside. 'Jack, is that you in there old chap?'

Mr Adams face turned white. 'Can't be....' The rifle lowered slowly until it was pointed at the floor.

'What is it, Mr Adams?' asked Molly. 'Who is he?'

'I say, Jack, it's me, couldn't come out here and give a chap a hand could you? I'm afraid I've gone and gotten myself terribly lost. Can't for the life of me work out what's going on.' The voice had a superficial friendliness to it. A cheeriness, even, but Molly heard something else underneath. It was an emptiness. A thinness. It wasn't a human voice; it was more like lots of sounds that had been mashed together to create the illusion of a human voice.

Mr Adams shook his head to bring himself out of his surprise stupor, and raised his rifle once again. 'Some sort of trick, this. A cruel trick at that,' said Mr Adams to Molly.

'I say, are you going to help me out or not? Dashed rude of you to leave me stranded in silence like this old thing.'

'Who is he?' said Molly.

'Cavan Scott. Least it sounds like him. Haven't seen the man in, well, must be close to forty years. Not since that awful business in the Amazon.'

'Jack? You still there are you?'

'We lost him, you see. One of my best men. One of my best friends. Never did find his body. Blame myself. I was in charge. My fault.'

'It's them, it's the Fisks, must be,' said Molly. 'We know it's you two out there! We're not stupid, you're trying to tempt us outside where you can get us! Is that what you did to the others? To Neil? To Billy Tyler? To my Mum?'

Molly blinked in surprise as she realised Mr Adams had his hand on the front door handle, his rifled lowered once more.

'Bally hell is the girl going on about, Jack?'

'What're you doing, Mr Adams?' asked Molly, as Mr Adams's face began turning red as he fought the urge to open the door and step outside.

'I'm in an awful pickle, Jack, could really use your help.'

Mr Adams began to turn the door handle.

'Stop! Stop it, now!' yelled Molly.

'Some... some sort of hypnotic suggestion, using me own memories against me....' Sweat began to bead on his creased forehead and he trembled violently.

'Open the door Jack, step on outside.'

'Fight it, Mr Adams!'

Molly pulled at him, trying to loosen his grip, but he was too strong for her. He opened the door. A man was stood on the pathway. He looked to be in his thirties and was dressed smartly in full explorer gear. Straw yellow hair was scattered atop his head, and a lopsided grin furnished his face. Mr Adams panted, catching his breath.

'At last, wondered what the hell was going on,' said the thing claiming to be Cavan Scott.

'I know it's not you, Cavan; I know a trick when I see it,' said Mr Adams, raising his rifle.

The thing placed a roll-up cigarette between his lips, struck a match against his boot and lit the end. Black smoke began to wisp around him. 'Ah, nothing like that first lung full, hey old man? Gets your senses bubbling and snapping!'

Molly wrinkled her nose in disgust as the creature inhaled and exhaled the foul, damaging smoke.

'Remember how you and I would stand out on cold nights and enjoy a smoke and a chat? Talking about the future.'

'I remember.'

He dropped the cigarette and rubbed it out with

the toe of his boot. 'I don't blame you. It wasn't your fault I died.'

'Shut up,' said Mr Adams, his voice a low growl.

'You listen to him, monster! Listen to him or he'll shoot you to bits!' said Molly, but the thing wasn't paying any attention to her, probably wasn't even aware of her existence. It had but one point of focus and one goal.

'You did everything you could have done. I mean, probably.' The thing shrugged. 'I still died, didn't I? So perhaps there was a thing or two you could have done better.'

'How dare you look through my memories, you filthy monsters. That's what I call unsporting behaviour. Now stand firm and prepare to die!' Mr Adams raised the rifle and looked down the barrel. The creature didn't appear worried, it continued to look at Mr Adams, gun raised and pointing in its direction, with the same easy, relaxed demeanour as before.

'Enough of this nonsense. Step outside, Jack. Come on old man, let's shake hands and forget the whole sorry affair. Share a smoke for old time's sake. Half-forgotten times and places, hey old man?'

The gun was still raised, stiff and steady; his hands did not tremble. 'I can feel you in my mind again, but I'm afraid I'm ready for you now. Caught me off guard the first time. Won't be taken twice.' Mr Adams pulled the trigger.

'Oh.' said Cavan Scott, a large ragged, bloodless

hole now where his forehead should have been. Molly could see straight through to the house on the other side of the street. Cavan Scott raised a hand as though he was going to say something, then crumpled to the pavement like an empty bag of skin, as though his bones and other inside bits had suddenly vanished.

'Good shot, Mr Adams!' said Molly, hopping from foot to foot.

'Damned rude monsters round these parts, trying to use a man's darkest memories against him.'

Molly stepped toward the pile of skin and clothing that used to be the pretend Cavan Scott and kicked at it gingerly with the toe of her shoe.

'Yuck,' said Molly. 'It's completely empty, like it was just a skin suit.'

Mr Adams reloaded his rifle and checked his harnessed twin revolvers. 'Some sort of puppet I'd wager, built from memories to try and tempt us outside.'

'Hey yeah, Gran said that we were safe in our own homes here in the Between; makes sense that they'd try to get you outside so they could attack.'

'Yep, though I get the feeling that this was merely reconnaissance.'

'What d'you mean?'

'They were testing, softly prodding us to see what sort of stuff we're made of. Won't be so easy from now on, not now they have the measure of our mettle.' Mr Adams patted Molly heartily on the shoulder. 'But don't you worry young 'un, we'll see the Fisks off alright.'

'You know you're going to lose, old man?' the skin of the creature that had pretended to be Cavan Scott said, attempting to smile. 'They're going to tear you apart and feed you to the bugs.'

Mr Adams lifted the skin with the end of his rifle. 'That so.'

'Oh, sure. No doubt about it. Be seeing you.'

Mr Adams swung the rifle and tossed the skin over the fence into the next garden.

'So,' said Molly, 'shall we go and say hello?'

Mr Adams smiled. 'Yes. They've made the first move; what say we get off the back foot and take the fight to them?'

Molly smiled and looked to her right, past the front of her own house and into the gloom-shrouded Fisks property. 'Time to enter the garden.'

~Chapter Eighteen~

Molly glanced up at the Boy's window, but it was empty. For a moment she wondered if someone had let him out, and if so were there now fresh red handprints decorating the walls of the corridor?

'Well, well, that's something.' Mr Adams was stood before the gate to the Fisks garden; as before, it had increased in size to loom over them.

'It's some sort of optical trick; it's not really that size,' said Molly.

'Tricky buggers, aren't they? If you'll pardon me French.' Mr Adams looked up at the sky. 'Seems somewhat darker on their patch too, hm?'

Molly nodded. 'Come on.' She led the way, shoving the giant garden gate open and stepping boldly over the threshold. Mr Adams smiled and strode after.

'Molly girl?' called Mr Adams, eyes blinking as he tried to get used to the sudden gloom, like someone had just turned the lights off.

'I'm here.' Molly touched his arm. Within a few seconds they had both adjusted to the darkness and could get their bearings.

'Like a jungle in here,' said Mr Adams, peering around at the giant, strange trees and the closely set greenery.

'Yes, only those little tree plant thingies over there? They aren't tree plant thingies, those are people.'

Partially covered by leaves and what might be a type of bark, eyes were visible. A nose. A mouth. 'It's macabre is what it is. Pure and simple. Whatever happens, we're putting these poor blighters out of their misery.'

Molly instinctively went to protest, but the words never came; she knew he was right. It was like her Gran had said, there was no saving these people now. Not now they were in the soil. They were sort of alive, but that's as alive as they ever would be; to try and reverse what had happened to them impossible. There was only this or death, and Molly knew there wasn't really two options at all, as leaving them in this state was disgusting. She and

Mr Adams would have to put them out of their misery, just as he said.

'Right,' said Mr Adams, done with examining the vegetation. 'Best foot forward; let's get to the house and find these monsters.'

Mr Adams strode forward with purpose, Molly looking at the nearest tree person face again before setting off after him.

They walked. The garden was different this time. Darker. Larger. More densely packed with people it seemed. Molly thought it must be the Fisks. Before, they had no idea she was coming; this time, they were fully aware and they weren't going to make it easy. They must be able to influence the garden in some way. Make it bristle at their intrusion.

They'd been walking steadfastly forward for almost half an hour now with no sign of the house bursting from the vegetation. Mr Adams hadn't paused, hadn't wavered; he'd marched at a steady determined pace directly forward, showing no sign of weariness in spite of his age. At times he even whistled, as though he was enjoying himself.

'Molly.'

The voice was a dry-throated whisper emerging from the gloom to Molly's right. She stopped and turned despite her better instincts. Silence. Molly turned back quickly to Mr Adams to follow on— only Mr Adams was nowhere to be seen.

'Mr Adams? Hey, where'd you go?' Molly half-ran, half-walked forwards, expecting to catch up with him at any moment. She'd only stopped for a second; he couldn't have gone that far ahead. 'Mr Adams!' She tried not to panic as she ran straight ahead, brushing aside leaves and branches that blocked her passage and whipped at her. 'Mr Adams! Where are you?!'

'Molly.'

'Molly.'
'Molly.'

'We see you.'

'We feel you.'

'Come be one with the soil.'

'Shut up!' Molly held her hands over her ears and tried to block out the swirl of voices that attempted to grab and smother her from all directions. Her heart jumped as she suddenly realised that each planted person she passed now had their eyes trained upon her, following her, imploring her to approach.

The Fisks had tricked her, made her take her focus away from Mr Adams long enough for the garden to swallow him up and take him away from her, and now here she was alone, the garden wanting her. Needing her.

That was when the trees began to scream.

All around her, the whole garden of tree people, their eyes and mouths wide, such piercing and unnatural screams that seemed to strike at her body, wearing her down, pulling at her so that it was like she was attempting to run through a swimming pool. Finally the garden had its way and exhaustion caused her to stumble slightly, to miss a step, and that was all it needed to bring her to the ground. Molly landed face first in the dirt, the impact winding her. As she fought to catch her breath she placed her hands onto the soil to push herself upright, but the ground in front of her was no longer solid and her hands sank almost up to her wrists.

Molly forced her body backwards, yanking her hands from the hungry soil and landing on her bum with her back against one of the screaming trees. She immediately knew that this was a mistake, but before she could throw herself to the side the branch arms cracked and grasped her, pulling her roughly to her feet so that her face was beside the tree's own face, eyes looking blankly at her, mouth screaming.

Molly kicked and tore at the plant but it felt nothing and cared nothing and did not give an inch, instead tightening its grip on her, hugging her closely, the rough bark digging into her skin through her clothing.

'Mr Adams! Help me! Help me!' she screamed, as weeds at the foot of the person began to snake upwards and wind around her ankles and calves. She could feel them begin to pull her downwards; they were trying to make her a part of the garden, make her like the other trees. 'No! Mr Adams, please!' Molly wriggled and fought but there was nothing she could do; the tree held her secure and the weeds had already pulled her feet down far enough that the soles of her trainers were now under the soil. Molly closed her eyes and thought of her Mum, of her waking and not being able to find her. Never being able to find her. Never knowing what had happened to her daughter.

A sound like a whip crack snapped out, and the branches holding her fell aside, causing Molly to topple backwards to the ground. Gasping, she kicked her legs, and the now lifeless weeds that had pulled at her broke with ease.

'You alright there, me girl?' Mr Adams stood over her, rifle in hand.

'I lost you,' was all that Molly could manage. She looked up at the tree that had almost killed her; where its head had been now resembled an exploded cauliflower. Mr Adams pushed it with the sole of one boot and it collapsed back onto the dirt, turning grey before crumbling like flaky pastry and blowing away on the breeze.

~Chapter Nineteen~

Molly regained her composure quickly. For the rest of the journey through the garden she walked with her hand gripping the hem of Mr Adams jacket. If they remained physically in contact then the Fisks wouldn't be able to play the same trick again. She hoped.

The tree people had stopped their screaming after Mr Adams had fired his shot and destroyed one of their number. The lack of screaming was a relief, but the fact that their eyes had remained open and watched them as they passed disturbed Molly. Were they spying? Accusing? Imploring her to set them free? Or perhaps they saw and thought nothing at all.

Either way, as she and Mr Adams made their way forward, all around them the wide eyes followed. Their gaze was steady, expressionless, empty.

'There's the chap!' said Mr Adams as they finally stepped out of the crowded vegetation and found themselves at last in front of the Fisks house. 'What d'you reckon then my girl? Circumspect or march in bold as brass?'

'Through the front door, bold as brass,' replied Molly.

'Like your style,' said Mr Adams, who checked his gun was loaded, then with a beckoning nod led the way.

The front door opened with a creak, Mr Adams rifle poking through into the corridor beyond. 'If you're there show yourself and face a reckoning!' said Mr Adams.

Silence.

The door was pushed open further and the pair stepped across the threshold. Molly shivered; the atmosphere was colder than before, like stepping into a fridge.

'What's that darned stench?' said Mr Adams, his nose wrinkling in disgust.

'It's the smell of death,' said Molly, grave.

'All right, bit melodramatic little one, chin up.'

'You's in our house now,' came Mrs Fisk's voice. Molly took a step back as Mr Adams swung the rifle's barrel from left to right and then up to the top of the staircase, but there was no sign of Mrs Fisk or

her husband.

'Playing silly beggars again are we, monster? Too afraid to step out and face what's coming to you?'

'The soil is hungry, Mr Adams. Oh, so very hungry and desiring it is for you,' cackled Mr Fisk.

'Come out here!' said Molly, sounding much braver than she felt. 'Come out here now, you bloody cowards!'

'What says you Mr Fisk, husband of mine? Shall we give the girl what she wants?'

'And spoils all our wicked, hell-ish fun, Mrs Fisk? I don'ts think so, oh no!' And the pair laughed, dry and flinty.

'Have it your way then,' said Mr Adams. 'We'll track you down to wherever you're hiding, like the craven cowards you are. We'll overturn your stone and then we'll dispatch the pair of you down into the fiery pit of damnation, you hear me monsters? Justice approaches! Can you hear the death knell strike? Listen for it, monsters, and listen well 'cos it strikes for you.'

Mr Adams eyes were determined, but a smile tugged at the corners of his mouth. 'You're actually enjoying this, aren't you?' asked Molly.

'This is me. This right here, right now. Action. Danger. Standing up for what's right. This is how I should have gone out, not old and put out to pasture to see out me days chewing the suburban cud. I should have wandered the dangerous walks of this world until me number was up or me ticker gave up the ghost and went kaput on me.'

'Died a hero,' said Molly.

'No, not as a hero, just as me. The real, fully formed me. What now then, Molly?'

She looked around at the deathly quiet house, her breath forming a fog in front of her face each time she exhaled. 'They're in here somewhere, hiding; we just need to check each room until we find them. And then....'

Mr Adams fondly patted the barrel of his rifle, as though it were an old family dog. 'And then it's my bullets turn to find 'em.'

They explored the ground floor first: the front room, the back room, the kitchen. They were all empty, yet Molly had the distinct impression that wherever they went, Mr and Mrs Fisk were watching them.

'There was a detached head in the fridge,' said Mr Adams.

'Yes,' replied Molly, remembering her first visit.

'Said I would die screaming.'

'It spoke to you? It didn't do that last time.'

'Yup. Bloody ghoulish it is. What next, down here?' said Mr Adams, tapping the door to the basement with his rifle.

'Let's try upstairs first; we don't want to go down in the basement unless we have to. There's no place to run to get away down there.'

'Smart girl. You'd have been a handy asset in my team you know. Good tactical brain that shows.'

Molly felt herself swell with pride a little as they left the basement's closed door and headed for the staircase. 'Also, it really stinks down there,' said Molly.

There were no bloody handprints on the stairs, or the upstairs corridor, much to Molly's relief. There were four rooms— three bedrooms and a bathroom— all empty. All completely empty. No beds or furniture of any kind, no carpet, no bath or toilet, nothing, all stark white and empty. Molly wondered if the same was true of The Fisks house in the real Awake world; did they only dress the downstairs to keep up appearances?

'Well that's that then,' said Mr Adams. 'Basement it is.'

'Not yet, look.' Molly pointed to the corridor ceiling. Mr Adams looked up to see a panel with a small, metal loop handle, large enough to fit a single finger through; it was the entrance to the attic.

'Not ideal,' said Mr Adams, as he reached upwards and pulled on the handle; the panel opened downwards and out folded a ladder. Mr Adams slung his rifle on its strap over his shoulder, spat on each hand and rubbed them together, then began to climb. Molly thought better of spitting on her hands before climbing after.

The attic, as they are wont to be, was dark. Dust hung thickly and unmoving; it made breathing unpleasant and scratched at Molly's eyeballs. 'Mr Adams?'

A click, and a weak, bare light bulb spluttered to life, barely casting enough light to illuminate a third of the attic space. 'Here I am, girl,' said Mr Adams.

A floorboard creaked in the gloom.

Mr Adams spun sharply, rifle pulled from his shoulder and into a firing position in one smooth, practiced step. 'Who goes there?'

Molly strained to try and make out any shapes moving in the darkened recesses of the attic, but it was useless.

'Fire a bullet into there, that'll move them,' suggested Molly.

'Waste of bullets shooting blind; you hold until you have eyes on a target.'

Another creak, this time accompanied by a wheezing cackle, caught their attention once again; Mr Adams pointed his rifle back and forth at the secretive gloom.

'Come out I say! Come, come. Only cowards hide,' said Mr Adams.

Nothing.

All was still and quiet.

'Right, then. Stay behind me Molly; time to advance into the dark.'

'But you don't know what's in there,' said Molly.

Mr Adams smiled. 'No, I don't.' He turned back to the darkened section of the attic and began to slowly step forwards, keen eyes scanning back and forth for any signs of life, for any signs of danger.

A sudden movement beneath her feet caused

Molly to take a step back in surprise. Had the floor just moved? 'Mr Adams, did you feel that?'

'Feel what?' replied Mr Adams.

'The floor, I think... is it moving?'

Before Mr Adams could answer, the floor lurched. It was like a cat arching its back, the floorboards thrusting upwards, splintering and cracking. It threw Molly backwards onto the floor and tossed Mr Adams, with a yelp, headlong into the dark.

'Mr Adams!' Molly stumbled back up to her feet as all around her the floor ripped itself apart. The floorboards beneath her cracked alarmingly, then split apart beneath her like a vicious mouth opening. With a cry more of surprise than fear, Molly fell into the wooden toothed jaws. As she fell through the hole in the attic floor, she braced herself to slam onto the altogether more solid floor below, only to find that it too had torn itself open and through she plummeted, down, down, down through the ground floor and towards the basement.

~Chapter Twenty~

It was dark and it stank. For a few seconds Molly lay still on the pile of soil that had broken her fall, and tried to stop her brain from spinning. She sat up and looked around her; as before, the piles of soil were dotted around the basement area. She looked up to the ceiling; through three ragged holes she could see Mr Adams, still in the attic, peering down at her.

'You okay down there, girl?' said Mr Adams.

'Yeah, I think so, are you?'

'Probably skinned me knees, otherwise all fine. You alone down there?'

Molly looked around again. 'Yes. Yes I think so.'

'Right, I'm coming downstairs. Hold fast!' Mr

Adams disappeared from view as Molly got to her feet.

As before the basement reeked of mould and decay; the stench was so strong it was difficult to breathe without gagging. Molly moved towards the stairs that led up to the ground floor; she had to get out of there, despite what Mr Adams had told her to do. She could feel it in her gut that this was the most dangerous place in the house to be alone.

'We sees you, Molly.' Molly gasped and stepped back; it was Mrs Fisk's voice.

'Where are you?' Molly turned in a tight circle, scanning the basement for signs of life.

'We is seeing you, Molly.' Mr Fisk now.

Molly ran for the stairs, for the exit, but before she could reach them the dark red, fleshy wall to her right bulged and tore. Thick, black gunk poured from the gash in the wall as two creatures stepped out and turned to face Molly, blocking her escape.

'Togethers at last, are we little Molly?'

It was Mr and Mrs Fisk, but they didn't look like the Mr and Mrs Fisk Molly knew from the Awake world. They stood twice as tall, their bodies a grotesque marriage of human and a tailless scorpion. They walked upon eight legs, sharp pincers snapped open and closed viciously at Molly at the end of long, thick arms. The only resemblance to the old couple to whom Molly had lived next door for years lay in their faces. They were stretched out and twisted, like they'd pulled on Mr and Mrs Fisk masks that were far too small for their heads. Their mouths were full of razor sharp teeth that chattered together as the pair wheezed and hissed dryly.

'Stay back or else!' Molly shouted.

The Fisks cackled and snapped their claws. 'Or whats exactly, little thing?'

'Or else I'll knock you out,' said Molly, raising her small fists.

The Fisks almost fell over laughing.

'Laugh all you like, but you're not putting me in your garden, not like Neil.'

'Oh girl, we is not going to put you in our lovely garden, is we Mr Fisk?'

'Oh no, no, and really no Mrs Fisk, our garden is too good for the likes of her,' replied Mr Fisk, 'What shalls we do instead then, wife of mine?'

'I really think instead we'll chop you all the way up and put you on the compost heap, that's the place for the likes of you.'

The Fisks laughed as they scuttled forward, claws snapping.

'Molly! Molly girl!' It was Mr Adams, rattling the basement's door handle, but try as he might it refused to open.

'They're in here! The Fisks are in here!'

Mr Adams was trying to shoulder-barge the door now, but it held firm and strong.

'Oh he can huffs and puffs but he won't get in,' said Mrs Fisk, a grin showing off rows and rows of pointed teeth.

Molly tried to dart past the pair to reach the stairs, but Mr Fisk swung out an arm and struck her in the chest with his claw, throwing her back onto a pile of soil.

'You wont's be going nowhere. This basement will be the last place you is alive in. The last place those eyes see before I poke 'em right out and chew on them.'

'Mr Adams! Help me!' Molly, winded from the hit, scrabbled backwards, but all too soon found herself against one of the walls, its flesh damp and sticky and disgusting as it seeped through her clothes and onto her skin. Molly wanted to run from it, but the only place to go was forward and that's where the Fisks were, moving with slow, deliberate steps, sharp teeth chattering, enjoying her fear. This was it. She'd failed. Determined not to go out cowering, Molly pushed herself to her feet and stood defiantly in front of the advancing Fisks.

'Come on then you pair of ugly idiots, come and get me!'

The Fisk's laughed and hissed, snapping their claws in amusement. 'Oh, brave one is it? Good, good; the brave ones always does the most screaming and crying in the end.'

'So much delicious screaming and crying and begging for mercy where none can be.'

'Now comes here, stupid girl. Comes and be torn apart.'

A shot rang out and Mr Fisk staggered back,

screeching, as his right shoulder spurted blood. The flesh walls surrounding them bulged and recoiled again and again as though the basement itself was in pain.

'You get away from her, monster!' Molly looked up to the hole in the basement ceiling; through it she could see Mr Adams, rifle now aimed at Mrs Fisk.

'Yeah, Mr Adams!' shouted Molly, punching the air.

'Did they hurt you?'

'No, I'm good, I'm okay.'

'Hurts! Hurts!' screamed Mr Fisk furiously.

'You shoots my husband, is it?' Mrs Fisk hissed with venom.

'For starters; now hold there and take what's coming to you, fiend.' Mr Adams fired at Mrs Fisk, but with unnatural speed she darted sideways, dodging the bullet. She scuttled with ease up the side of the flesh wall and across the ceiling, reaching a clawed arm through the hole and grabbing Mr Adams ankle, yanking him forward. He tumbled through with a cry of surprise, landing heavily onto the same pile of dirt Molly had earlier.

'Mr Adams!' Molly dashed towards him.

'My rifle!' Mr Adams pointed to where it had fallen. Molly broke off to try and reach it, but a clawed hand snatched it up.

'Maybe I shoots holes in you and your old body now, hey?' said Mr Fisk, yellow gunk oozing from his shoulder wound, brandishing the weapon at Mr

Adams.

'Go ahead, monster, you don't frighten me, shoot away,' said Mr Adams.

Mr Fisk laughed, before crushing the rifle in his claw as though it were made of cardboard, then tossing the now useless, crumpled rifle aside. 'I is going to take you apart, old man. Tear you to tiny bits. Piece by fleshy, bloody piece. You will screams and beg for death, but you won't get it, not for months and months.'

Mr Adams reached for his belt on which were holstered his twin pistols, but Mrs Fisk had scuttled down the wall behind him and she grasped him painfully by the wrist in one of her claws, lifting him up off the ground like he weighed as much as a bag of sugar.

'Unhand me, beast!' Mr Adams shouted, his face twisting with pain.

'Naughty, naughty old Mr Adams.' hissed Mrs Fisk, taking the pistols and crushing them in her spare claw, 'You wont's be doing no more shooting in our house.' She tore the gun belt from around Mr Adams waist and threw it into the dark.

'Awful manners you has, trying to kills your gracious hosts,' said Mr Fisk.

'Put him down, you're hurting him!' said Molly.

'That's all that's left for him and for you now, girls; hurting!'

Mr Adams shook his spare arm and a thin blade slid from his sleeve. Grasping it tightly, he thrust the knife quick and hard into Mrs Fisk's arm, grunting with the effort. She screeched in surprise, dropping Mr Adams to the floor. The flesh walls convulsed once again as Mrs Fisk recoiled in pain.

'Few tricks up me sleeve yet, monster!' said Mr Adams as Mrs Fisk batted the knife out of her arm and kicked it aside.

'No arms up your sleeves soon though, not after I pluck 'em out!' screamed Mrs Fisk, and she swung one of her claws at Mr Adams, striking him across the head and sending him sprawling to the floor, unconscious.

'Mr Adams!' Molly moved to help, but the flesh wall behind Mr Adams split like an open wound and a thick tendril uncoiled and wrapped itself around Mr Adams unconscious body like a python, dragging him into the wall itself and out of sight.

'Bring him back! What is that thing doing to him?' Molly demanded.

The Fisks laughed and they laughed. 'Keeping him safe for laters. You be the starter, then onto the old man for main course, yes? He may be olds, but so tough, so strong, he will stand up to a lot of punishment and fear and pain, and we have so very much of all three waiting for him. Now come here, weak little thing, come here now.'

Molly looked around desperately as the Fisks scuttled towards her. She dove to one side as a claw swung, trying to grasp her by the neck. Molly rolled and found herself next to Mr Adams knife, slick still with Mrs Fisk's yellow blood; she grabbed it. Looking up she found Mr Fisk looming over her and tried to roll aside, but he was too quick, wrapping his claw around her neck and lifting her up before him like she was nothing but a bug, ready to have its legs pulled off to see how long it could live without them.

'Has you now, filthy child, we has you now.'

Molly grew red in the face as the squeezing claw made it difficult to breath. She kicked out again and again but was too far away for her short legs to connect.

'Looks how it wriggles and struggles, oh wife of mine. So desperate it is to cling to its small and meaningless life.'

'Pluck, that's what she has, you know, to come to our house, our true house that is. To come here and stands toe to toe, brave as you like. Pure pluck that.'

'Oh yes, yes, pure pluck it is. Talking of pluck, which eyeball shall I pluck out first with me sharp, sharp teeth? The left or the right?' And the Fisk's laughed a dark, vicious laugh, Mrs Fisk slipping loose a long, forked tongue to lick hungrily at her lips.

Molly was growing dizzy as Mr Fisk pulled her closer, his jaws opening wider and wider to expose ever more teeth. She waited, and she waited; she thought the panic might overwhelm her, but she stayed still and waited for her moment. A few inches more and she was ready. Knife grasped firmly in hand she struck out, driving it up to the handle into one of Mr Fisk's eyeballs.

An explosion of thick, black ooze shot from the injured eye and over Molly's face. Mr Fisk staggered back screaming, releasing Molly to fall several feet to the floor.

'Gets it out, gets it out!' Mr Fisk thrashed his head back and forth in agony as Mrs Fisk rushed to his aide.

'Evil girl! Stupid girl! We rip you apart now! We make you hurt!' screamed Mrs Fisk as she held Mr Fisk still and pulled the knife from his ruined eyeball. It emerged with a further torrent of gunk gushing out after it, Mr Fisk falling backwards in pain, the flesh walls convulsing in sympathy.

Molly looked around for something to defend herself with, anything at all, but the floor was empty but for soil. At least she had done some damage; at least she had gone out fighting.

Mr Fisk stood tall, black blood cascading from his eye socket. 'Kill you! Stupid girl! Kill you! No more waiting, no savouring, I am killing you right now!'

Molly would not step back or cower, would not give them the satisfaction; she would go out brave and without screams. She thought of her Mum. She thought of her Dad. 'Come on, then! Kill me you disgusting, evil creatures.' Molly stood her ground, eyes wide, defiant, and waited for the end.

'No.'

The voice was calm.

Even.

It spoke with assured authority.

It was a voice Molly recognised.

The Fisks stopped and turned to the basement door, which was now open. A man stood framed in the doorway. He was unnaturally tall, dressed all in black, and his head was entirely missing a face but for a mouth.

'Our house!' shouted Mrs Fisk, as she and her husband backed away from the Tall Man, as though they were frightened of him. Molly had never seen the Fisks frightened before.

'You have no rights!' Mr Fisk hissed petulantly.

'You will not kill this girl. She has already lost so much for such a small thing.'

'Yes! We has her! Kills her! This is our house!'

'You will not kill anyone. Not anymore.' The Tall Man raised an arm towards the back wall; its flesh tore open and Mr Adams toppled out.

'Mr Adams!' Molly rushed to his side, helping him stand as he wiped gunk from his clothes.

'What on Earth happened? One minute I'm fighting, next minute, nothing,' He looked up to see the faceless man. 'And who the bugger is that?'

'They is ours! Our house! They attack us in our own home. Have pity on us,' said Mrs Fisk.

'I pity you. I do not have pity for you. Girl, man, come here to me now.'

Molly and Mr Adams skirted around the fuming

Fisks and hurried up the staircase to join the Tall Man.

'You are finished now. Finished here,' said the Tall Man to the Fisk's.

'Is that so, is that really so?' said Mrs Fisk.

'Maybe's... maybe's we come for you perhaps? Hm?' said Mr Fisk at the Tall Man, growing bold.

'Maybe we do that very thing. You could be lovely in our garden. Such a rare bloom.'

And the Fisks began to cackle as their fear receded.

'Do you want to play a game?'

It was a small voice.

The voice of a child.

The voice of a Boy.

'It's him, the Boy from across the road!' said Molly.

'No! No, can'ts do this to us! No!' the Fisk's spat accusingly at the Tall Man.

'I can. I have,' he replied, matter of factly.

'What shall we play first?' asked the boy, 'How about... finger painting?'

In a panic the Fisks ran up the walls, towards the hole that would lead to the first floor, but as they reached it they found the Boy there, stood upside down on the ceiling, blocking their way.

'I only want to play,' said the Boy. 'You're going to be my new playthings. He said I could have you. For as long as you last, anyway. I always break my toys, you see, in the end.'

'Help us!' said Mr Fisk to the Tall Man.

'Help us now!' said Mrs Fisk.

'No.' He replied.

The Tall Man ushered Molly and Mr Adams out of the basement. Molly stole one last look at the Fisks as they fell to the floor and cowered from the Boy, as he calmly walked down the wall towards them.

'I need some paint. Do you have some for me?'

The Tall Man closed the basement door, cutting off the awful sounds within. He reached into his mouth and pulled out a large brass key, turning it in the basement door's lock.

'You keep a key in your mouth?' said Molly.

'Of course not. I keep it in one of my stomachs,' he replied, before swallowing the huge key as though it were a pea.

~Chapter Twenty-One~

Molly, Mr Adams, and the Tall Man stepped out of the Fisks' house and into their garden, or what was left of it. All around them the vegetation, human or otherwise, had wilted and collapsed to the ground. Vivid greens turned brown and black as they decayed rapidly before their eyes.

'It stinks out here,' said Molly, correctly.

'There is an odour,' agreed the Tall Man.

The trees and the planted people flaked and peeled away as a strong wind brushed the garden clean, leaving nothing but bare soil. The garden was its normal size again too, now that the Fisks control had vanished.

'Very decent of you this, old chap, to lend a hand, but d'you mind filling me in a little? I mean, who the Devil are you? Look a bit like a monster if you ask me. Not that I'm prejudiced, mind you,' said Mr Adams.

'I don't have a name. I've never needed one,' replied the Tall Man. 'I am from here. I am Lord of here. Of Between. I suppose you would call me a guardian. Of sorts.'

'Royalty, hey? Well I'm used to that; dined with Kings and Queens alike I have in my time,' said Mr Adams.

'Thank you for helping us,' said Molly.

The Tall Man turned his faceless head to her and nodded. 'You are welcome.'

'But why now? Why didn't you help all the other people who were put in this garden? Why did you let the Fisks do this?'

'It is their house, their property,' he replied.

'But you helped us. You helped me.'

The Tall Man nodded. 'Yes. I had spoken to you. So much loss for one so young. So I helped.'

Molly wasn't sure that was a good enough answer, but she was too tired to argue, too happy to have rid this place and her street of the monsters, too eager to leave it behind and go home to her Mum. Go home to the real world.

'Well, thanks,' said Molly.

'You are welcome,' said the Tall Man.

'Come on, then, Mr Adams, time to wake up.'

Molly set off for the garden gate, but Mr Adams didn't follow. 'Mr Adams?'

'Ah, right, yes.'

'What's wrong?' asked Molly.

'Well. You see. Thing is, I thought I might just stay here.'

Molly looked at him in silent surprise for a few seconds. 'What? Stay here? Between? Like, forever?'

'Yes. Well, no, not forever. Just until I pop me clogs,' he replied, smiling.

'But don't you want to go home?'

'That place isn't home, not for me; it's just where I was waiting quietly for the Grim Reaper to pay me a visit, and he was taking his bloomin' time, let me tell you, girl. My future was all behind me. All used up. But here? Well, here is fresh, unexplored territory. Monsters roam this land. Just the place for me to walk me final days.'

'Adventure,' said Molly, smiling.

'Exactly!' said Mr Adams, clapping his hands together. 'Adventure is life, Molly girl. At least, it is to an old duffer like me. In the real world I die a clapped out old husk, but here? Well, here I can go out as me. The real me.'

Molly looked into his eyes and knew he was making the right decision. She ran to him, arms open, and hugged him tightly.

'Thank you, Mr Adams. Thank you for risking your life. Thank you for being the bravest person

I've ever met. Thank you.'

'Thank you for giving me a second chance at living,' said Mr Adams.

'Molly?'

They turned to the source of the voice. Stood in the dead garden was a young boy, around eleven years old, a pair of glasses perched on his nose. He was also grey. His skin, his hair, even his clothes. 'Molly, Mr Adams, what's happening? Why doesn't that big tall person have a face?'

'Neil!' Molly bolted forward and embraced her friend.

Mr Adams clapped his hands together in delight, 'Well fancy that.'

'I never thought I'd see you again,' said Molly.

'What? Why not? What's going on here exactly anyway?'

'You know this ghost?' said the Tall Man.

'This is Neil. Neil's my friend. The monsters took him and put him in their garden,' Molly replied.

'What did he say? Did he call me a ghost?' asked Neil.

'Ah, yes, well a bit good news-bad news, this young Neil, m'lad. You see, on the one hand, you're dead. Monsters done for you, I'm afraid.'

'Oh.'

'But look, you're still around, you still exist,' said Molly.

'Yeah. I suppose so.'

'Just look at you!' said Mr Adams. 'You still talk

and walk and smile and frown and think! P'raps a bit on the drab looking side, bit gloomy grey, but you're still up and kicking, hey?'

Molly leant forward conspiratorially. 'How's it actually feel? Being dead, I mean?'

'Well. I dunno. I don't really feel dead. Not that I know what that feels like, so maybe I do feel dead.' Neil looked around him at the familiar surroundings. 'Is this Heaven then? I thought it would look a bit better than your street.'

'No.' said the Tall Man. 'This is not Heaven. This is my land. This is Between.'

'Between Awake and Asleep is Between,' said Neil. 'Oh, that's right, isn't it? I don't know how I know that, but it's right.'

'That is so.'

'Well Molly, you best be on your way, hm?' said Mr Adams.

Molly nodded and turned sadly to Neil.

'I can't go home, can I?' asked Neil.

Molly shook her head, then lunged forward to hug him before any tears forced their way out. 'I'll always remember you, Neil, and think of you as my best friend, but I need to go back home. Go to the Awake world and to my Mum.'

Molly stepped back and smiled at Neil, who smiled back, pushing his glasses up the bridge of his nose once again. 'Yeah. I know. I'll miss you though.'

'Don't worry, I'll look after the lad,' said Mr

Adams. 'How'd you like to be my apprentice, hm?'

'Your apprentice?' said Neil

'Well, me number two, brothers in arms. Me, the grizzled, seasoned explorer. Adventurer, hero, brave as you like. And then you, me brave, faithful, second in command. What say you? Ready for all the daring adventures you can swallow? For thrilling close scrapes that'll make the hair on your head stand on end? Ready for a big old slice of saving the day on a regular basis?'

Neil looked at Molly, then back to Mr Adams. 'Well, I suppose I'd normally be scared of all that, but seeing as how I'm already dead, I don't see I could have much to be scared about.'

The Tall Man smiled but said nothing.

'I've got to go,' said Molly. 'Thanks so much for everything. I'll never forget any of you.' With one last look at Mr Adams, and a nod of the head to the Tall Man, Molly ran. She ran for the gate, twisting once to wave without looking back, arm stretched up high. She ran to her house. She flung open the front door and bounded up the stairs and into her Gran's room. Gran was stood waiting for her, arms open; Molly dove at her and hugged.

'They're gone. They're dead. The Fisks. The monsters. Everyone's safe now,' said Molly.

Gran stroked Molly's hair tenderly and smiled. 'I knew you could do it, my clever, brave child. There's lots of me in you, you know. Fight and spirit. We shouldn't be afraid of the monsters, not the likes of me and you, oh no; the monsters should be afraid of us.'

Molly let go and smiled up at her dead, grey Gran. 'I suppose I better go then, back to the real world. Back to Awake.'

'Yes. The Awake world is for the living. Though I understand Mr Adams thinks otherwise. Good for him I say.'

'Will I see you again?' asked Molly.

'Oh, I should think so. In dreams. I'll always be in here.' Gran tapped Molly's head with her finger. 'Now, go on. Go to your Mother. Go live life, my fearless one.'

As Molly went to lay down on the bed, she paused, 'Gran?'

Her Gran stopped in the doorway, turning back. 'Your Father.'

'Yes,' said Molly, quietly.

'He is so very, very proud of you,' said Gran, and she blew Molly a kiss.

***

Molly was awoken by somebody calling her name.

'Molly?'

Molly rubbed at her eyes and sat up as her Mom entered Gran's room.

'There you are, fallen asleep on Granny's old bed again, have you?'

Molly smiled the biggest smile anyone had ever smiled. She leapt off the bed and ran at her Mum, almost bowling her to the floor as she wrapped her tightly in her arms.

'Careful, what has gotten into you?' asked Mum.

'Nothing, I just... I love you,' said Molly.

Mum smiled and held Molly close, brushing her hand tenderly over her hair as her Gran before her had done. 'Silly sausage. Love you too. Though having just said that, I suddenly remember I'm supposed to be angry with you, after the way you spoke to the poor... to those two....' Mum trailed off, confused.

'What is it? What's wrong?'

'Can't quite remember what... you were rude, is that it? To someone?'

'Just to the Fisks,' said Molly. 'And trust me, they deserved it.'

'The Fisks? Who are the Fisks?'

Molly blinked twice. 'The horrible old couple.'

'Oh. That sounds familiar. I think.' Mum shook her head, as though dismissing her confused thoughts. 'Come on, let's go and have some breakfast.'

'Yum,' said Molly. 'I'm starving'

'Oh, you know, I hear they might finally have a buyer for next door. Be good to have some neighbours at last. I didn't like having an empty house next door.'

Molly went to say something, but then thought

better of it. The Fisks had gone. Now let them be forgotten.

Molly and her Mum walked downstairs together.

***

The Boy stood sulking as the Tall Man shut him safely away within the confines of his room once again.

'You know I can't let you play as you please, Boy,' said the Tall Man, but the Boy didn't answer. The Tall Man straightened the note that was attached to the door, a note he'd written oh so many years ago. Satisfied, he made his way along the blood coated corridor, the air heavy and metallic, down the white carpeted stairs, and out into The Between.

~Chapter Twenty-Two~

But that's not quite the end.

A week passed, perhaps more, and Molly found herself sat on her front door step, playing cards alone, an empty house to each side of her. She missed Neil. She missed Mr Adams. But she was safe now. Her Mum was safe. No one else would be taken away by the Fisks. No more children removed from their beds, their souls to be feasted upon.

She turned card after card, placing them carefully down.

The Fisks old house still stood empty. It was in the process of being bought, but the new owners had yet to appear.

Molly gathered up the cards and placed them into their box.

A movement to her right, a ghost of a twitch in the corner of her eye, caused Molly to stop and turn to the fence that separated her front garden from the Fisks' property. Molly squinted but could see no signs of further movement.

Placing the box of playing cards down, she approached the fence and looked over into the garden. Not that it looked like a garden any longer. It was devoid of any vegetation, just paving stones dotted across dark soil.

Molly looked left and she looked right, but there was no movement to be seen. A cat, perhaps? Molly thought not. She turned and walked back to her house, making her way to the kitchen. From one drawer she retrieved a small torch, from another a carving knife. It was heavy and cold to the touch.

She made her way back outside and walked to her gate; exiting and turning right, she walked to the Fisks' garden gate. Of course the gate was of normal size. She pushed it open and stepped inside. Molly looked ahead to the house and was sure she saw something dart out of view from one of the downstairs windows. Nothing distinct, a flash of pink.

Molly closed the gate behind her and made her way through the barren garden and towards the front door. She tried the handle. It was open. She went inside.

'Hello?' her voice echoed around the empty house, but no reply was forthcoming.

Molly began to make her way from room to room. The whole place had been gutted. No furniture, or carpets, walls stripped back to the plaster.

'Is there something in here? Come out, come out...'

Next she made her way upstairs. She checked each room, the bathroom void of tiles, or even a toilet, and then clambered up into the attic, shining her torch into every gloomy, hidden corner.

Lastly she stood on the stairs that lead down into the basement, running her hand along one wall. Brick. It did not react to her touch; it wasn't warm, or damp, or fleshy. Just brick.

'Oh, well. I suppose I must be imagining things,' said Molly loudly to herself.

She turned and left the house, swinging the carving knife up and down with each step, certain that if she turned sharply back to the house she would again see a flash of pink as something ducked from view in a window.

***

Molly sat up that night cross legged on her bed, the carving knife gripped tightly in her hand, waiting.

She left her bedroom door open.

Nothing came.

Molly knew something was playing games; she also knew she wouldn't be able to stay awake forever.

The next night she found herself nodding as she waited and had to pace up and down the room to make sure she didn't fall asleep.

'What is wrong with you?' asked Mum, as Molly lay asleep at breakfast, spoon in hand, face on the table.

The third night was more difficult still. Molly was very sure she had drifted in and out several times without even knowing it, chunks of time suddenly disappearing. How much longer could she last? How much longer would the thing wait before making its move?

The fourth night fell, and so did Molly's resistance. She tried as hard as she could, pinching herself sharply, jumping up and down and pacing the room, but eventually, without even knowing it, a deep sleep took her.

'Mo—'

...

'—en to m—'

...

'Wake up—!'

'Gran?'

Molly's eyes fluttered; she'd fallen asleep she realised. As they fluttered, her eyelashes brushed against something. It was wrapped around her face. She opened her mouth to shout and the thing that was wrapped around her face surged forward, forcing its way past her lips, past her teeth, past her tongue, choking her.

She couldn't breathe!

Molly kicked and tore at the thing that clung to her, that wrapped around her, that enveloped her. Her thoughts began to static around the edges and her chest convulsed as it fought for air, air that was denied it by the awful 'thing' that was killing her.

'No Molly,' said Gran, looking down at her, eyes fierce. 'Not like this; fight for goodness sake! Fight!'

With a sudden show of strength, Molly managed to pull an arm free. She grasped the terrible thing and tore it from her, ripped it out of her throat. It squealed and thrashed in fury as she freed herself from it and threw it into a darkened corner of her bedroom.

Molly scrabbled backwards on her bed, gasping for air, her vision flashing red. She looked around, but there was no sign of her attacker. She found the knife under the duvet, where it had fallen as sleep took her.

'Come out, then. It is you, isn't it? Come on now, you had your chance, no use playing games anymore.'

For a few seconds there was silence, the only noise Molly's heartbeat as it thump-thump-thumped in her ears.

Finally, the intruder shuffled forward from the shadows and into sight. At first it was difficult to make out exactly what it was that scrapped, and rolled, and weaved into the light. It looked like a creature deflated. Without solid definition. Like the bones and organs within had been gotten rid of and all that was left was an empty, useless suit of skin, teeth and hair. It was like Mr Adams's friend, the pretend version of Mr Adams's friend, after he had shot it. Only this was a different pretence. This had once been an old person who tended to their garden and made cheery, boring small talk with a young girl.

'Hello, Mr Fisk. Or is it Mrs Fisk?'

What was left of one of the ancient pair reared up. The part of it that had once covered a skull weaved back and forth like an adder emerging from its basket at the request of the snake charmer's flute.

'Wicked girl. Evil girl.' The voice was but a grating whisper. How this remnant could even speak, Molly did not know.

It was unclear by the voice which of the monstrous pair it was, not that it mattered. Part of one of them had survived. Part had clung on to some vestige of existence. Nothing so very old and so very, very evil could be extinguished in one fell swoop without leaving some of itself behind.

'Hello.'

'I survives.'

'No, I don't think you do. Not really, anyway.

This is just what's left of you. A sad old thing holding on as best you can. But you're dead, really. More or less. Might as well give up.'

Molly stepped forward; the thing reared back and up, like it was attempting to stand up onto its feet. The eyeholes had collapsed into empty, cruel slits, and the mouth hole stretched wider and wider still, jagged, uneven teeth dripping with a thick, white-red liquid.

'You let me see you, correct? You wanted me to know you were there. To come looking for you. To fail.'

The thing said nothing; it just weaved back and forth, back and forth.

'You knew I wouldn't be able to sleep then, not with you out there, waiting to come in here and get me. That I would stay awake, waiting, and that eventually, if you were patient, I'd not be able to resist any longer. That I'd fall into a deep sleep that I wouldn't wake from as you crept in and suffocated the life from me.'

The thing's mouth stretched wider and wider still, so wide Molly thought it might be able to swallow her in one.

'I will kills you, evil girl....'

'No,' said Molly. 'I don't think you have the strength to do that. Not anymore. That's why you wanted to sneak in and take your chance after I had fallen into a heavy sleep. You knew that I'd be able to fight you off if you came at me any other way.'

Molly took another step forward; the thing staggered back. It fell, sagged, tried to right itself.

'Alright, enough of this now, you're beaten,' said Molly, and she strode towards the pitiful, evil thing as it slid back against the wall. Molly lifted up her knife and with stroke after stroke chopped the creature into tiny pieces. Once done she emptied a box of pens, pencils and pads, gathered up all the pieces of it, and dropped them into the box.

She carried the box downstairs into the kitchen; opening a drawer, she found some old matches. She could feel the pieces of what was left of one of the Fisks moving and banging against the sides of the box.

Molly made her way into the back garden and placed the cardboard box onto the grass. Within the box, all the yellowy-pink-brown pieces wiggled like worms, coiling around each other, some pieces becoming whole again as the creature struggled to make itself whole.

'Look how you wriggle and struggle. So desperate to cling to your small and monstrous life,' said Molly.

She lit a match and dropped it into the box. Within seconds, the container and its contents were engulfed by strong, orange flames. The remains made no noise, but in her mind Molly could hear it screaming. Cursing. Begging. Threatening.

'Shush now,' said Molly to the flames, and soon enough the noise in her mind stopped.

Once the box was burned to ash, Molly stamped out the remaining embers, yawned, and went back inside to sleep.

And to dream.

ABOUT THE AUTHOR

Matthew Stott writes strange stories. Originally from a place in England so far north that it used to be Scotland, he now lives in London.

@mattstottwrites | mrmatthewstott.com
Facebook.com/matthewstottauthor

Please consider leaving a review wherever you bought the book, or telling your friends about it, to help spread the word.

Thank you for supporting my work.

~Look Out For More Tales From~
~Between~

The Identical Boy
The Increasingly Transparent Girl

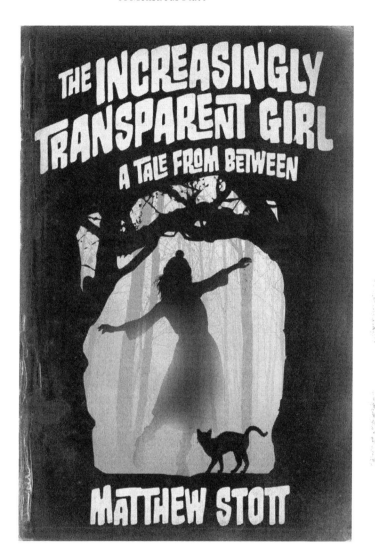

Made in the USA
San Bernardino, CA
11 December 2016